The Storyteller of Cotehill Wood

By Kathleen Boyle

ISBN: 9798637056422

© Kathleen Boyle. April 2020

All rights reserved. No part of this publication may be reproduced,
distributed, or transmitted in any form or by any means,
including photocopying, recording, or other electronic or mechanical methods,
without the prior written permission of the publisher,
except in the case of brief quotations embodied in critical reviews and
certain other non-commercial uses permitted by copyright law.
For permission requests, email the publisher at the address below.

Disclaimer

This is a work of fiction. Names, characters, places and incidents either are products of
the author's imagination or are used fictitiously. Any resemblance to actual events or
locales or persons, living or dead, is entirely coincidental.

Cover image: Smstudioinc

E: kathdodd@aol.com

About Kathleen

Kathleen Boyle (nee Dodd), was born in Liverpool, England, where she spent her childhood years before leaving to train as a teacher in Hull in 1972. Kathleen has worked as a teacher in Hull, Leeds, London and Carlisle, and at international schools in Colombia, Bahrain, Cairo, Armenia and Vietnam. She has written stories and poems throughout her life, and published a collection of poems about growing up in 1950s Liverpool entitled, *Sugar Butties and Mersey Memoirs*, as well as a collection of poems for children about a teddy bear called *Harry Pennington*. During her time in Bahrain she wrote *The Pearl House*, a short story which spans the cultural divides of Liverpool and Bahrain. The story, together with her poems, *Bahrain* and *Umm Al Hassam*, were published in the collections; *My Beautiful Bahrain* and *More of My Beautiful Bahrain*. Kathleen has written a series of children's stories for Beirut publishers Dar El Fikr, two of which, *The Jewel of the Deep* and *The Magic Pearl and Dilmun*, have now been illustrated and published. Kathleen has also contributed to the poetry and short prose collections, *Love, Travel, Lonely* and *Happy*. In 2015, while teaching in Cairo, Kathleen published her novella, *Catherine of Liverpool* and completed a revision and Part 2 of the story during her years in Armenia, where she was Head of Primary at CIS Armenia. A mother of three and grandmother of two, with a home in Cotehill, Cumbria, she has given author presentations in Russia, Armenia, Vietnam and Liverpool. She is currently teaching at SIS Binh Duong in Vietnam, where she wrote *The Storyteller of Cotehill Wood*.

Dedicated to
Pat and Marg

Prologue

New York, January 2020

Fionuala, just a quick email to say It was good to Skype chat with you today. Your mum and I were pleased to hear all is going well in England, and excited to know you plan to visit Cotehill and the Cottage, after all this time.

Before you left last year, you asked me about life in Cotehill woods: I think you implied that it must have been boring to live in a remote cottage, deep in a wood, so I decided to write about it for you and anyone else interested in the strange events that occurred during my time there.

Here it is!

Sit back, relax and enjoy the read...

Much love,

Dad

Chapter 1

The Cottage in the Woods

It all began a long time ago, in the 1970s, when I was a youngster, just setting out on life's journey with no clue what was to become of me. All I knew was I wanted to tell stories, but the universe seemed to have other plans.

'Tell stories? Over my dead body!' My father had exploded. 'The family business is where you're going son. Stories, my eye!' He would never be won over, I'd always known. 'And it's time you had a haircut and threw out those old jeans.' Dear old dad. He had never understood much about me, but deep down I knew I wasn't family business material, and so did he. I had no interest in plastic packaging. Apart from anything I was a Friend of the Earth, and the business went against everything I stood for. Sad, but true, as they say.

In those days I was living in my granny's cottage deep in Cotehill wood. She had sadly passed away, but on the bright side had left me her cottage. It was cosy and felt safe because I had spent a lot of my childhood there.

'One day all this will be yours,' Granny had told me over supper one night, while the full moon watched through the kitchen window. 'This cottage is full of surprises young Donovan. You'll be happy here.' She was the happiest person I've ever met, with the brightest smile and twinkling green eyes. I had inherited those eyes, as well as the cottage, together with her red locks, although by the time I was around they were white.

My college friends thought it was pretty cool for me to own a cottage and, as it was isolated, we had great parties there with no-one to complain about the music. Sometimes we'd build a bonfire and camp out in the garden and I'd practise storytelling on them. It seemed the right thing to do, but they were less enthusiastic.

'Give it a rest, Don,' Simon burst in one night when the whole gang were gathered. It had been one of those perfect hot August evenings and we'd chilled to a few heavy metal tunes. The stars came out and I thought it was the right time for a story. Donning my special storytelling top hat, I began...

'Once Upon a Time ...'

'Give it a rest, Don,' Simon said. We don't want to hear your dumb stories anymore.' I tried to stay cool, although deep down I was crushed. I remember a dreadful silence befell the group and we all stared into the flames until the embers glowed and Simon said; 'Time to go.'

They clambered into his Deux Chevaux. My girlfriend, Lisa squeezed my hand, and I remember feeling totally destroyed. She whispered in my ear; 'He's right, Don. Time to put the stories to bed.' And off they drove, leaving me to pick up the empties and dowse the flames.

It was then that the strangest thing happened; well almost the strangest. But before I tell you about that, I need to explain something about my granny.

Granny was a very small woman, no more than three feet in height, so that by the time I was seven years old, I was taller than her. Mum was a tall woman, but the small gene apparently emerged from time to time in the family it seemed, and my great, great granddad had it. Granny remembered him, and would tell me stories about how hard he worked to chop the wood and build the cottage, which was then hers, and now mine.

'He never stopped grafting, my granddad,' she would say.'He'd look at me with his big green eyes and say; *"One day this cottage will be yours, Indigo, and you'll be no taller than me, so I'm making it with you in mind. The big ones will have to fit into your world."* And that's why the cupboards are low and the doors so small.'

It didn't seem strange to me because I'd known it from childhood, but my friends were always surprised when they first visited. Tall people felt like giants in my place. I'd tried to adapt the furniture to fit me, so it was comfy enough. Granny had a picture of Great Granddad Seth, which she kept on the sideboard in the living room. I'd left it there out of respect, and also because after listening to Granny's tales I felt I knew him.

So, there I was clearing up after my friends and wondering how they could be so cruel, when a voice from behind me says. 'You need a new repertoire.' Taken completely by surprise, I spun round, only to see no-one there. 'Down here,' said the voice and, looking down, I saw a very small man who looked a lot like my great, great granddad, but scruffy. He was dressed in ragged clothes, had a mass of shaggy red hair and a long red beard.

'What the... ?' I yelled, raising the branch I was using to clear the ashes. My first thought was that I was hallucinating, but the small man held his ground. Then, totally against all my non-violence principles, I brought the branch down on his head, but it went straight through him.

'No need for that, Don,' he said without flinching. I threw down the branch, ran for the cottage and once inside, slammed the door, scared out of my mind. 'I just want to help. That's all.' He was there, inside, sitting comfortably in Granny's chair. 'Chill out, Don. I'm not harmful, but thought you might like some good advice. I heard what your friends said and must say I can't blame them. Your stories are old and worn now. You need some fresh material. Trust me, I'm here to help.' He waved his hand, inviting me to sit down. These were the days before mobile phones, otherwise I'd have been messaging my girlfriend like crazy. Instead I calmed down and listened.

I've no idea how long he stayed, but he talked until I fell asleep. I recall waking up at daylight and there was no sign that he had ever been there. Strange dream, I thought.

Chapter 2

The Hat Trick

Weeks later, I had got myself a gig telling stories at the library in Carlisle. It was summer break, the kids needed entertaining and I needed money. My rich dad had more or less disowned me and I had to eat, so decided to advertise myself as a storyteller and use a few old Cumbrian tales and a song or two. Lisa met me in town and we had a coffee at Watts.

I'd brought my top hat along, decorated with a few wild flowers from the hedgerows and some red ribbon. 'Your hat looks good,' Lisa said. 'Let's hope the stories live up to it.' She laughed, but I wasn't amused.

'Some encouragement would be nice,' I thought.

'Once Upon a Time... ' I began when the children had settled. 'In the days of King Arthur and his Knights, there was an old hag in a forest who wanted a husband.'

'What's an old hag?' asked a smart boy on the front row.

'An ugly old woman,' I answered, smiling at him.

'Like Mrs. Frith?' he said, causing hilarity amongst my audience. Mrs. Frith, who was the librarian, cast me a ruffled glance, but the damage was done, I couldn't undo it, and every mention of the old hag reduced the children to helpless laughter, and Mrs. Frith turned redder and redder. Then, just as I thought her head was about to explode, a remarkable thing happened. They fell silent and paid attention; watching me and listening with deep concentration, as I told of the knights who refused to marry the old hag and the one who agreed, in order to save the kingdom.

Then I played them a tune on my tin whistle, and it

was over. They thanked me and told their mums and dads how amazing I was.

'Cool hat trick,' Lisa said, as we sipped coffee at Watts again, before I headed home on my scooter.

'Yeah thanks,' I grinned. 'Wait a minute; what hat trick?'

'The changing colours one. How did you do that? Even the flowers changed. Amazing! You grabbed the kids' attention, Don. Good for you.' I said nothing. What could I say? I had no hat trick.

Despite the Mrs. Frith incident, the gig was a success and the woman herself seemed happy enough as she gave me the envelope full of money. No mention of the insult. Once home, I threw some beans into a pan, and bread in the toaster. Life was good!

It was while clearing the plates before going to bed that I came across the note. I had scraps of paper all over the place; being a storyteller involves jotting ideas and story titles whenever they pop up. I try to be organised and keep a filing cabinet and alphabetical system, but I would scribble the idea on whatever scrap of paper was around at the time, and if it reached the filing system, it would be lucky. In that regard, I have changed little. So, the note was in the cutlery draw, and it was not one of mine.

Chapter 3

The Note

It lay in the cutlery drawer, a two centimetres square piece of luminous paper which glowed pale green, and upon the paper the words;

REMEMBER OUR DEAL

In old style script. 'Our deal?'

My first thoughts were of Lisa, but I couldn't recall a deal we'd made. I picked up the note to scrutinize it and, as I pondered the beautiful script and the strange glow, it disappeared, leaving me holding thin air and gasping with disbelief. Sleep didn't come easy that chilly September night. A deal? Remember it? I didn't, and the disappearing note was creepy. I thought about phoning Mum to tell her about it, she was good at putting my mind at rest, but it was late now, almost midnight, and dad would explode if the phone woke him.

So I phoned Lisa.

'A glowing note that disappeared?' she mused after I'd told my story.

'Yes', I nodded to myself.

'Don!' she said, 'you woke me up to tell me this? I have work tomorrow. Mrs. Frith at the library gave me a Saturday job. I have to be up at seven o'clock. and you wake me to say you found a luminous note in your knife drawer which disappeared?'

I knew she was angry; her voice was getting louder with each word. 'Yes, Lisa. I did. So what do you think?' I won't go into her response. After she hung up on me I felt alone. Sitting in the big chair, the only one I fit in, I racked my brains for a clue. Great, Great Granddad watched me from his portrait on the sideboard and I stared back. The most frustrating thing was not having the note to stare at. I drifted off to sleep, and in my sleep I heard a voice which was familiar, repeating over and over; *Remember our deal, remember our deal...*

A loud banging woke me. There was someone at my door. I tumbled out of the chair and in a state of half sleep, pulled back the bolt and peeped out. It was becoming hard to predict what might happen, but I had a vague recollection, from my dream and needed to make a note before it slipped through the net and out of memory's grasp.

'What the...?' I groaned, peeping through the part-opened door and meeting the angry glare of my dad.

'It's ten a.m. my boy!' he blurted.

'Thanks for the update,' I replied, feeling a little confused that dad had driven all the way to my cottage to tell me the time.

'The factory!'

'Factory? What factory?' I responded nonplussed and searching the cabinet drawers, desperate to find paper and pen and write down my dream memory. Dad stood watching from the doorstep.

'My factory!' He continued, still in bellow mode.

'Dad, I don't understand why you're here shouting at me about your factory. Come in and sit down, I'll make a brew.'

He entered and looked around my living room. 'How can I sit in a chair made for a three year old child?' he sneered.

'It was made for a three foot high woman, dad. My grandma!' I was getting angry. I'd found a scrap of paper, but needed a writing utensil.

'Why are you scrabbling around?' he blurted.

At last I spied a pencil at the back of a drawer, and scribbled my memory onto the scrap of paper, which just happened to be an unopened envelope.

'There you are!' Dad said. 'That's the reason!' Thinking he was referring to the dream recollection I'd just penned; I was full of surprise, as you can imagine. Dad was now sitting in my chair. The only one big enough to fit a tall adult, so I perched on one of the tiny stools dotted around the room and met his glare.

'You know something about this?'

'Yes of course I do. I sent it,' Dad expostulated. He was red in the face.

'YOU sent it? YOU sent the tiny glowing message?' He twitched and became suddenly quiet.

'What?'

'The disappearing message about the deal.'

'Jumping Jehoshaphat, Donovan! What are you talking about? I sent you that letter in your hand about starting work at the factory today. You should have been there at eight a.m. with the other work experience people. We waited for you! You're my son and your absence was an insult to me and all I've worked for. This is your future, Donovan. Your future is wrapped in plastic! But here you are rambling on about glowing, disappearing messages. I worry about you, Son. Wait till your mother hears this one.'

For a moment it felt like all the joy, fascination and hope of life was sucked out of me, but I held my breath and counted to ten.

'Dad, sorry I didn't open your letter. Must have missed it somehow. Didn't I tell you Mrs. Frith at the library has taken me on as a storyteller, Saturdays and Wednesday evenings? I thought I'd mentioned it, Also I thought I'd mentioned that I'm not interested in working in the factory. I don't see my future as being wrapped in plastic; quite the opposite actually. Now I have to get ready for my storytelling session, if that's okay with you.'

After a few more rants dad left with the parting shot; 'And get a haircut!'

I smiled benignly as he drove off in the Merc. and returned to my dream memory, which required some deep pondering.

Chapter 4

Footprints in the Ashes

As I mentioned, all this seems a few lives away now, and I smile to myself when I recall those days when only I knew the truth and the truth was so strange, that even I questioned it.

~

After my angry Dad's departure, I returned to the scribbled dream memory. *Footprints in the ashes*. Then I tried to recall more of the dream content. Had someone spoken the words to me? Had I seen them written? Was it an image in the dream? I dressed and packed for the storytelling session at the library, aware that I wasn't well prepared, but hoping to wing it this time, on the back of my previous success. My scooter, Ivanhoe, was parked close to the bonfire pit, and I was busy squeezing the top hat into the under-seat space, when I noticed them. On the ground where I stood, as clear as daylight, were a set of tiny footprints embedded in the ashes of our bonfire, and in a flash of recollection I saw him standing there, heard his voice; 'You need a new repertoire.' Saw him on my chair in the cottage and remembered the conversation.

'Jumping Jehoshaphat!' I heard myself exclaim. Using the envelope with my dream scribble, I captured an image of the dew damp footprints, then sped off through the woods to the library in Carlisle, all the while wondering what the deal was and if there were consequences for my not sticking to it.

'And the pixie told the princess she must guess his name, and if she got it right all would be well, but if she didn't then terrible things could happen.' The children shifted impatiently.

'Rumplestiltskin!' called a little girl.
'Yeah, Rumplestiltskin is his name!' The others agreed.
'Can we have another story?'
'Can you do that thing with your hat again?' Deflated, I struggled to the end of the session with Mrs. Frith looking on, grim faced. Lisa avoided eye contact. When the disappointed children left, Mrs. Frith gave me the cash and a warning; 'Don, I think we'll give it another try, and if your performance doesn't pick up, I must let you go.'

This was a worrying development. I was still paying the instalments for Ivanhoe and needed the extra cash from the library gig. Also, there were no more gigs on the horizon. College resumed in a few weeks, and I'd have the allowance from Mum and Dad, but until then the cash in my pocket had to stretch a long way.

Lisa and I went for a coffee and silently sipped. There was too much on my mind; tiny footprints, the little man, the disappearing glowing note, and a deal. I couldn't help thinking my failure today had something to do with not sticking to the deal, but how could I do that when I had no idea what it was? Lisa didn't believe a word I was saying.

'The hat thing was great, Don. Why did you leave it out this time?' she asked, still avoiding eye contact.

'Because the hat thing was not my doing, Lisa. It was some sort of magical intervention.' She gave me that look that suggested I needed psychiatric treatment. I re-told the story from the top, and this time pulled out the envelope on which were the little man's footprints. Lisa examined them and I sensed the germ of belief.

'Show me these, Don,' she said, and in no time at all we were on our way.

Ivanhoe sped through the woods like a winged horse, and to my huge relief the footprints had remained in place.

'You see, Lisa! Just as my dream told me. Footprints in the ashes.'

'Don, these are so strange,' she said, now on her knees for a closer look and peering at the set of prints. 'If these are genuine, then I have no choice but to believe the rest of your story.' She stood up and gave me a hug, which I needed. Life's lonely when the world turns against you.

We went for a long walk in the woods and tried to make some sense of a nonsensical situation. 'You must wait and see, Don.' Lisa concluded as we parted company at her house in Cotehill. 'Let's just see what happens next.'

I didn't have to wait long.

Chapter 5

Conan the Brownie

It was a lovely autumn evening and the walk back through Cotehill wood, knowing that Lisa believed me, lifted my mood. The deal thing worried me though, and it felt like I was at a disadvantage, since I hadn't a clue what the deal was.

Back at the cottage I made a cup of tea and lay on a blanket in the garden watching the stars emerge and the rosy glow of sunset fade.

'Sorry, Don. I should have turned off the memory eraser after our talk the other night. It happens sometimes.'

Some seconds passed before the penny dropped, as they say. I turned my head forty-five degrees away from the stars and found myself staring at the tiny man. Surprisingly, I remained calm.

'What's your name?' I asked, deciding to extract more information before he disintegrated.

'Conan is my name, Don. I came to help you out a bit with the storytelling malarkey. You could do with a few tips. We made a deal when I last came, and I was miffed because you forgot to keep it, then Poppy suggested I may have erased your memory, so I checked the records and that's exactly the case, so I beg your pardon, Don, hopefully we can start afresh.'

He was smaller than I remembered, maybe two feet in height. He had a long straggly beard and looked as if he'd been burrowing through the earth most of his life.

'What are you, Conan?' I asked coolly.

'I'm a brownie, according to your fairy mythology, but to me I am what I am. Anyway we haven't much time…'

'Who's Poppy?' I demanded.

'She's a fairy. Now, Don, hear me out. If you help us find Timothy, you'll get your reward, but if you refuse, then you'll end up working for your dad and wrapped in plastic, hahahaha.'

'Not funny, Conan. Who's Timothy?'

'Timothy Ogden is a storyteller. The best, I might add. He travelled the country telling his tales, and we fairy folk would go along with him. We'd have a fine time. Then he vanished. It was after a gig, as you call it, at Allonby on the Solway Coast, years ago. My time's almost up. Don boy, listen closely, whenever you spend time on the search for Timothy Ogden, you'll be rewarded, but if you don't bother, your future is in plastic fantastic. Haha.' With that, he disappeared, leaving behind a strange odour of eucalyptus, like the woods in midsummer.

Remember, this was the '70s and there was no such thing as Internet in those days. The word Google had different connotations then, so tracking down information could be laborious. Apart from a strong desire to avoid the fate of the plastic factory, I was genuinely intrigued by the weird carry-on and decided it was time to put cynicism aside and take a serious approach to Conan's quest for Timothy Ogden.

Mum called in on the Sunday after the Saturday library disaster, which was also the day after my chat with Conan.

'I've brought a few treats for you, Donovan; chocolate chip biscuits, peanuts and fruit. I'm guessing you buy little fruit, but you mustn't forget the vitamins.' She glanced around the living room and I waited for the nostalgia trip. The cottage was her childhood home. Her eyes teared up. 'Such happy memories, Don,' she said. 'Did I ever tell you about the times your granny brought a troupe of actors to the woods and had them stage a play for us? They had us singing and dancing along with them, I can see them now. A real jolly bunch.'

'No, I don't think you did, Mum. Were they from Carlisle?'.

'No, they'd come over from Bassenthwaite way. I remember she called them the Bassenthwaite Troupe'

'Sounds like a lot of fun. She was quite a woman was Granny. I'll put the kettle on for a cuppa.'

'That'll be nice, Donovan.' She sat in the big chair and I

perched on a stool while she reminisced. She'd had quite a childhood in the cottage.

'Mum, have you ever heard of a man called Timothy Ogden? He was a storyteller around these parts I believe.'

'Timothy Ogden?' She pondered, sipping her tea, and I watched her gentle eyes drift into deep thought mode. 'No, never. There was a Timothy Threlkeld in the village a few years ago, but can't recall any Ogdens. Why do you ask?'

'I'm interested in his work; they say he was very good, but seems to have disappeared.'

'Hmm, I'll ask around for you. Must go now, son. Your dad asked me to say hello and he'll see you on Wednesday at the factory. He's hoping to pick up a big new order for disposable food trays and would like you to be in from the start.'

'Tell him I'm busy Wednesday, and for the rest of my life.'

Mum smiled as she left the house. 'I'll let him know. Oh, he also asked me to tell you to get a haircut.' We both laughed, while she clambered into her little yellow Mini and was soon Cotehill village bound.

As I closed the door, my phone rang. It was Simon the insulter. I hadn't seen or heard anything from him since he suggested I desist from storytelling.

'Hi mate! How's it going?' he chirped as if he hadn't deflated my ego just a week ago.'

'Simon! All's great with me, mate.' I tried to sound pleasant.

'Mate, about that night, sorry, I was out of order. Anyway, to make amends, I got you a gig at a folk club near my place. They were advertising for a storyteller, believe it or not, so I told them I'm your manager and got you a booking for tomorrow night. You need to go get your act together old pal.'

Chapter 6

The Quest Begins

The Blue Moon Folk Club was tucked away down a narrow alley in the old quarter of Carlisle. Simon was waiting for me at the door. I had decided on a King Arthur story for the evening, together with a few tin whistle tunes. There were two singers before me, and a lot of cider being downed by the jolly crowd. I recall feeling nervous. 'Are you sure they want to listen to a story?' I whispered to Simon who was singing along merrily.

'Too right they do mate. You'll knock 'em flat.' I was wondering if it was a setup; Simon's little joke at my expense.

The audience was very merry by the time they announced me, and I donned the top hat with serious misgivings. I began the tale of King Arthur and his sojourn in Cumbria. Looking back, I can only describe what happened next as magical. For the next hour it seemed as if fantasy was our reality. Time was of no importance and my audience seemed spellbound as I told the tale and played the tunes. When it was over there was unanimous appreciation and huge applause. It flabbergasted Simon.

'Well done, Don!' he exuded, slapping my back repeatedly. 'They love you! Great hat trick!' His surprise suggested I'd been right with my suspicions, but deep down I was pretty surprised myself.

'Thanks to my manager, Mr. Simon Hill,' I said slapping him on the back in return, and deciding not to dwell on the hat trick comment.

My manager fixed up another gig for the following week and, by the end of the evening, our little fireside fall out was history.

'Oh, one thing before I leave, Simon; have you ever heard of a guy called Timothy Ogden?'

'Never,' he replied.

Ivanhoe carried me home like a magic carpet. A huge blue moon hung in the sky, and in the wood an owl swooped past so close I could have touched it. Tucked up in bed and still excited by the success of the night, I was sure I heard Conan's voice just before dropping off to sleep.

'You did well, Don,' he said.

Chapter 7

The Deal

'Timothy Ogden, Timothy Ogden,' Lisa repeated thoughtfully. She was working in the library and I'd gone along to keep her company and do some research around the question of Tim. Lisa was flicking through the Dewey system cards in the filing cabinet. 'Do we have any dates to go by, other family members? Anything at all that might help?'

'Not much, really. Only that he went missing after a gig in Allonby. Conan said he was well-known as a storyteller and considered to be the best at his craft.'

'Who's Conan?' Lisa inquired.

'Ahh, I replied,' realising she wasn't up to scratch with events. 'I'll tell you over coffee.'

'A brownie?' she mulled, sipping coffee in the gloriously coffee scented Watts. 'Yes, Conan's a brownie,' I nodded. 'It seems he forgot to block the *erase memory spell* after he spoke to me on the night of the bonfire, resulting in my having no recollection of the deal we made. If Poppy hadn't reminded him, I'd still be under the dark cloud of no deal consequences.'

'And who's Poppy?' Lisa tentatively asked.

'A fairy,' I replied.

'And the no deal consequences are?' she ventured.

'A lifetime in plastic,' I grimaced. She looked puzzled, 'Dad's factory.' I clarified.

'Ahh, I see,' she nodded sagely. 'Donovan,' she began sounding like my mum, 'only because I saw the footprints in the ashes, do I believe you. I will cast all doubts aside and go with you on this one. So it seems we need to find a trail to follow and locate Timothy Ogden.' Her lovely brown eyes glistened with enthusiasm. She looked every inch the librarian with her long black hair tied back and granny glasses perched on the end of her nose. I was very grateful for having her in my life and took her hands in mine.

'Thanks for believing me, Lisa.' I whispered, knowing she was the only person on earth in whom I could confide.

'OK, Don. I'll trawl through some newspapers and other records whenever I get the chance. Mrs. Frith might know something. I'll ask her. Can you come in tomorrow?'

'I'll try, but Dad wants me to spend the day at the factory. Not sure I can escape that,' I replied.

I couldn't.

The factory day came and went. Dad was insisting I join the business when I finished college. 'I want you to look after the new ready meal packaging department' he said.

'Do you know a guy called Timothy Ogden?' I responded.

'Is he in plastics?' he asked.

'No, he's a missing storyteller' I answered. Silence ensued.

Back at Cotehill woods, I walked through the autumn and revived my senses before heading to the Greyhound Inn in the village to meet Lisa for a game of snooker.

She'd been doing a lot of research trawling through books and encyclopaedias at the library. 'I looked up brownies. They're household spirits that come out at night while you sleep and do housework. You're supposed to leave a bowl of milk by the hearth for your brownie. They can be easily offended.' Lisa was clearing the snooker table in her usual adept manner, as she spoke. 'Also, Mrs. Frith knew an Ogden family; went to school with Matilda Ogden, but doesn't recall Timothy. She thinks they moved to Keswick a few years ago.'

Well and truly beaten at the pool table, I paid for the drinks and we sat in the snug, mulling it all over, wondering if Granny had left milk out for Conan and whether the Ogdens were still in Keswick. We decided it was time to search farther afield. Sunday bus rides to Keswick and Allonby seemed inevitable.

Back at the cottage I began to plan for the gig and pulled out my collection of stories file. Granny told us lots of stories and whenever I found the time, I'd write one down, trying to remember the detail Granny used because I wanted to re-create the magic she conjured as I listened in total awe.

'Remember the Long Meg stories, Don?'

Conan was perched on the mantelpiece beside Great Granddad Seth's picture. I was startled, but kept my cool.

'Hello Conan. Yes I do, now you mention them.' Legend had it that Long Meg was a witch who danced with her daughters in a field near Penrith, and was turned to stone by a wizard, together with the rest of the coven. Granny and mum took me to see the stone circle, which is amazing. She would weave many a tale around the story of Meg, embellishing it with names for the other witches and how and why they were dancing on the day they sealed their stone fate.

'Good stories Don, worth re-visiting.' He was right. They'd be perfect for the Blue Mooners. 'Your Granny Indigo did a great job with Meg.' He disappeared, leaving me staring at the floral wall.

Simon was waiting for me at the Blue Moon. He was taking his role of storyteller manager seriously. 'You're my pot of gold, Don, pal; a treasure chest lying in a dark cave waiting for the key to arrive and reveal its glorious contents. Think of me as the key to your success, Donovan. This is only the beginning of our long and winding road to success.'

Funny how tables can turn, but I tried not to be cynical. after all, Simon had found me a much-needed source of income, and I could carry on paying the instalments for Ivanhoe because of it. Life in the woods would be impossible without my scooter.

Long Meg and her Daughters went down well with the punters at the Blue Moon Club, and the tin whistle seemed to have a life of its own that evening. I even got an encore!

Chapter 8

A Breakthrough at Allonby

Allonby on a sunny day is a delight to behold. The sea licks the sandy beach and seagulls chase the fishing boats ready for a tasty meal. The sweep of the shoreline from Silloth to Whitehaven along the coast is pure poetry, and I hope that one day I will be able to visit again.

Lisa and I planned to call in at a few shops and inns to ask about the elusive, mysterious Timothy Ogden, but first we had a picnic on the beach. The bus journey had been long, and we were ready for the fresh air and open space of the seaside.

Lisa had a plan of action and our first stop would be the Post Office; 'Post Office workers know everything and everyone,' she informed me.

The place was as tiny as a postage stamp and we could hardly fit inside together.

'Well, now,' Mrs. Sloan, the postmistress, began. 'We had a few places that used to hire storytellers, and still do for that matter. There's the Old Horse Shoe across the street, and the Star and Dragon just over the bridge. Sometimes the Village Hall Committee would organise an event. We've had some good ones.' She advised us to start with the Star and Dragon because it was open.

I recall our excitement as we set off, feeling sure we were soon to solve the mystery, but sadly, although we visited all the places suggested by Mrs. Sloan, Timothy was unknown.

There was a small van parked in a layby selling soft drinks and sandwiches. Walking brought on a thirst, so we stopped for refreshment. Taking a chance, I asked the old man, who could barely see over the counter, if he knew anything about Tim.

'Timothy Ogden, he muttered. Ogden is a name I know; big family, but I've never heard of a Timothy. What does he do?'

When I told him, his face lit up. 'Storyteller! Yes, I know him. They called him Toddy Oggy, if I'm right in thinking. Yes, Toddy Oggy. Toddy Oggy, the tale spinner. He was a great one, was Toddy.'

Lisa and I exchanged bemused glances. It turned out that our Timothy had been around Allonby and district twenty years ago, telling stories wherever he went. 'Folk won't remember him as Timothy Ogden. He was known far and wide as Toddy Oggy,' our informant continued. 'Disappeared though. Just stopped coming round and I've often wondered what happened to him. He knew every imaginable story did Oggy, and every inch of Cumbria. He'll be in his 50s now, same as me.'

So it seems our quest was doomed from the start. Lisa complained about all the wasted time she'd spent in the library looking for Timothy. I reminded her she worked in the library and there wasn't much else to keep her busy, but I had to agree, Conan had led us down the wrong path.

We retraced our steps in search of more information on Toddy, but although it was now obvious that he was well known in his day, the story was always the same; he had disappeared without trace from the Allonby scene.

Our bus came trundling along and we had to leave, but the journey had been worthwhile. It was a great day out, and we now knew exactly who we were looking for.

Chapter 9

Small Fragments

It was mid-September and life after our Allonby trip became very full. Two weeks of the holiday to go before term started in October, and Simon was working overtime to promote my storytelling career, not without success it must be said. He would tootle through the woods in his 2CV with his diary of dates and venues, so that we could plan the details of my future gigs. Amazingly, he had bookings right up to Christmas. My dream was becoming a reality, and I'd sit in the garden until sunset trawling through my story files and planning the weeks ahead, knowing that once college resumed, I'd have other stuff to think about.

Also, I had a few encounters with Conan, mostly as I worked in the garden and usually to give me some advice. He was apologetic for misleading me over Toddy's name. 'We all knew him as Timothy, Don. That's what we called him and so did your granny.' Another bombshell.

'You mean to tell me Granny knew Toddy?' I rounded on him, but he'd disappeared. He had a habit of delivering profound information before vanishing. I was becoming accustomed to that, but it was deeply frustrating.

Thinking back to that time, Conan was a frequent visitor, and I'd usually make a few notes of our conversations. He loved to talk about Indigo, my Granny, and also mentioned the Bassenthwaite Troupe. I recalled Mum's fond memories of them and made a note that Lisa and I should go through to Keswick one Sunday, and Penrith, where Long Meg and her daughters languished in stone. Conan once talked about a man called Michael Scott, a wizard from Scotland. Just a brief mention, but I made a note of it to follow up some time. It's all so obvious to me now, but the mystery of Toddy's whereabouts seemed unsolvable.

On a brief visit to Mum and Dad's in the village one Saturday, I asked about Timothy again. 'They also knew him as Toddy Oggy,' I told them as we sat around the table enjoying one of Mum's signature quiches with chips and salad. Dad drew a blank, but Mum came up trumps; 'Toddy! Yes!' she gushed. 'I remember him. He came to Granny's often. A magical man, Donovan. His stories would carry us away to other worlds, truly a great storyteller. So he's the Timothy you've been looking for?'

Mum gave me a detailed description of Oggy who, it transpired, was unusually tall and very skinny. He would wear a green and black pin-striped suit when telling stories and, like me, used a tin whistle and top hat. He would tell stories about the fairy folk around Cumbria and beyond, and the traditional stuff like Little Red Riding Hood.

'It was so long ago, Donovan, but now I think about him, he was a very special man. I wonder what happened to him.'

After lunch I called at Lisa's house, but there was no reply; I had a lot to tell her, so phoned later that day. I was hoping we could catch the bus to Keswick the following day. Walking back to the woods, I noticed a chill in the air. October was coming and soon my days would be filled with college. My thoughts panned the events of that week as I tried to piece together the small fragments of information we had gathered. Where was Conan trying to lead me?

These were the fragments as I saw them:

Keswick and Bassenthwaite Lake
Allonby
Cotehill woods
Granny
Michael Scott
Long Meg
Me
Conan

I sensed that somehow these were connected, but had no idea how or why. At the cottage I made a few more notes and tried to phone Lisa, but strangely, there was no reply.

Ivanhoe carried me swiftly to the library story gig, which was a great success. The numbers were increasing every week, and Mrs. Frith began to wonder if I should do more sessions, but I wasn't so sure. She didn't know where Lisa was. It seemed she hadn't been to work that day and also, worryingly, hadn't called in with an explanation.

After the library I met Simon for coffee and discussed the future plans. That evening I'd be at the Blue Moon, and I decided I should ask about Toddy while there amongst the story enthusiasts.

The session went well. I told the Old Northumberland tale of Dragon Castle, we had a few regulars from the east coast, who appreciated the nod towards their rich story culture.

There was standing room only that night as the line-up was good with one of the most popular local groups headlining. At the end of my tale I asked the audience if anyone had ever heard of a storyteller called Toddy Ogden, or Toddy Oggy, or Timothy Ogden. There was a murmur of thoughtful consultation and nodding amongst the ranks which seemed promising.

'I'll be sticking around for an hour or so.' I said. 'if you know of him I'd appreciate the info.'

Simon congratulated me with his customary slap on the back and a pint of my usual lemonade on ice. 'You're on fire, Don boy, and the hat gets me every time! How do you do it?'

Before I could ask him what went on with my hat, apart from it being an old topper decorated with a few late autumn leaves, a couple of regulars interrupted us.

'Well done lad,' Stan said, shaking my hand. 'Funny you should mention Toddy, we'd just been saying how like him you are. Not so much in looks, but the act. You've got the same way about you, even the hat thing, how it lights up and that.'

That was when I had a lightbulb moment, so to speak. Conan had done something to my top hat; the thought was one of those flashes of an idea that could be lost if you don't write it down, so I whisked out my pen and notepad and wrote: *Conan hat?* Then returned to my informers.

'When did you see Toddy, Stan?' I asked, pencil poised at the notebook, like an eager reporter, hungry for news.

'He came here all the time back in the '60s. Tall fella, wore a hat like yours and did the same trick with it. Coloured lights and all. Sometimes I swore I saw a fairy or two when he was telling his stories, but my wife thinks it was the cider playin' tricks on my brain.' He was in a reverie of remembrance and his friend Archie backed him up.

'Stan, mate, I'd back you up on that one. I saw them too, a little guy dressed in green with long red hair and beard and a fairy in a red dress, used to sit on his shoulders and dance on his arms when he played 'is tunes.'

Hiding my shock, I pressed on. 'When did you last see Toddy?'

'It was some time in the '50s here at the Blue Moon. I recall he seemed glum and his act wasn't up to much that night, No fairies or magical hat tricks, but a sad tale... He was going to Allonby the next day, he told us he'd see us next time and that was the last we saw of him. Never cem back.' *Cem* is the Carlisle word for came. We have our own dialect there, which you wouldn't understand if I used it too much, for instance, *eed* means head, *areet* means all right, but I'll continue in the language you will recognise, although now and then you may find I slip into Carlisle speak.

We talked for a while longer, after which Simon and I left, and he walked with me to where Ivanhoe was parked.

'Mad men!' he laughed. 'Mad as hatters! Fairies and little men. Really? Somehow I don't believe a word they say. Too much cider, eh mate?' He looked at me expecting agreement, but I was stony faced, wondering who the fairy could have been.

Chapter 10

Poppy

It was late when I reached the woods and drove slowly along the narrow, winding road that led to my cottage. There were deer around and it sometimes happened that one would leap out of the darkness in front of me. In the trees, owls perched, watching for the slightest movement and their eyes glowed in the headlights. The woods were alive at night. As I reached the cottage, I heard the phone ringing, (we only had land-line phones in those days) and raced to catch it, thinking it might be Lisa. It was.

'Hi, Don.' She said.

'Where the heck have you been, Lisa? You had me worried.' It transpired her granddad had died suddenly, and the family took off to Devon in the dead of night on Thursday.

'I couldn't phone you because hardly anyone has a phone down there.' She sounded tired and upset, so we arranged to meet the next evening. I hung up and noticed Conan perched on the dining table.

'Don, my friend. What a performance tonight! I came to congratulate you and brought a friend along. Thought it was time you two met. Poppy, come out now.'

From behind the milk jug on the table, the tiniest little being appeared, dressed in bright red with jet black hair. I peered down at her and drew closer for a better look. Mesmerised by the sight.

'It's so rude to stare, Don. I thought better of you,' she said, in a small, but clear voice. My mouth was agape and eyes wide. Not a word could I say.

'Don, we can't stay long. Poppy wanted to meet you

and say thanks for trying to find Timothy, er... Toddy.'

'Yes, Don, I know you're doing your best and in return we're helping you out with the act. What do you think of the hat trick? Timothy loved it. We miss him so much. You know he used to write to your granny, whenever he went travelling, such interesting letters,' she said, hauling herself up the jug and sitting on the rim.

'Time to go, Poppy.' Conan said, rather abruptly.

And they were gone.

I stared at the jug for some time in disbelief. It was one thing hearing the old lags at the Blue Moon talk about seeing a fairy, and quite another actually seeing one, although I mused that if Conan the Brownie can become an everyday occurrence, why not Poppy the fairy? It was as I was dropping off to sleep, I realised that what Poppy told me was hugely significant to our quest. Toddy wrote letters to Granny. Were they still in the cottage? If so, where could they be? I would begin the search after a good night's sleep, but little did I know what would happen that night.

In my dream there were black horses galloping across moorland, they were hot and steamy from the distance they'd run. Galloping, galloping and steaming from the nostrils. The sky was leaden, and the moor, grey. I was thinking about Conan and Poppy in her red dress perched on the milk jug and the letters from Toddy to Granny, while the horses pounded the earth.

'Donavan,' I heard in my dream, 'Donovan, sweetheart. Can you hear me?' It was Mum in my dream. What was she doing there? I opened my eyes and was staring at a brightly lit ceiling. Not my cottage. I gasped and my head ached. Slowly, to my dismay, the story of the past week unfolded. How I hadn't arrived to meet Lisa and wasn't answering the phone. How Lisa came to my cottage and found me lying in the garden beside Ivanhoe. How she ran to call my parents and an ambulance and how I had spent the past week unconscious in a hospital bed.

'Now what?' I asked.

'Rest,' the doctor replied. 'At least a month.'

I was physically and emotionally shattered, although realised how lucky I was that Lisa found me. I had no recollection of getting out of bed, let alone leaving the cottage and heading for Ivanhoe. It was as if I was trying to go somewhere. Or had I already been?

Lisa hadn't examined the scene, she was in a panic and acted as fast as she could to get help. For the next few days I drifted in and out of sleep.

Chapter 11

A Mystery Malady

The doctors couldn't diagnose my illness. They tested me for everything they could suspect, but nothing showed up. Neurologists, bacteriologists, ear, nose and throat specialists and every other *ist*, but they found nothing. The week college started, I was still in hospital. The college admin was OK about it and said I could start late and catch up. Business Studies and English Literature were now on hold.

Mum and Dad were hardly ever away from my bedside, Lisa came every evening, and Simon brought the gang in from time to time. Gradually I regained my strength and appetite.

My parents wanted me to move back in with them. Mum was worried that it might happen again and Dad saw it as an opportunity to wean me away from the storytelling and lure me into plastic.

'Come home, son. The cottage can be your retreat now and then, but your mum will be happy if you come home for a while at least. I've got big plans for the factory and need you to be involved. Plastic's the future, Don.' I declined, but agreed to Mum visiting every day and staying over now and then for her peace of mind.

The day I left hospital I was still weak and wobbly, but on the mend. Lisa and Simon had organised a surprise welcome home event at the cottage. It was mid October and chilly, so they had a bonfire burning and blankets for me to wrap up warm. The gang were there, and Mum brought a huge pan of chilli con carne with garlic bread, straight from her kitchen.

There was a lot of concern, because my sickness

remained undiagnosed, and there was a fear that it may return. Admittedly I was worried and frightened by the suddenness of it, and couldn't help feeling that what happened was part of the mystery jigsaw I was trying to piece together. The black horse dream remained vivid in my mind. Where was I going that night? Or where had I been? I needed answers and felt sure Conan and Poppy had them.

Lisa moved some of her stuff into the cottage, so she could monitor me. She'd been back at college for two weeks and was already busy writing an essay. In those days that would involve writing by hand unless you were lucky enough to have a typewriter, which neither of us did. Lisa had a bike with a basket she'd pile her college books in and peddle off to lectures each day. I had arranged to return to college early November, so I had some time to rest and recover at home. Mum called in everyday to check on me and bring food. She arranged for some logs to be delivered by one of the guys in the village, as I was too weak to chop wood as yet and winter was drawing in.

Simon had cancelled my gigs until mid-November, so my thoughts began to drift back to stories. I planned some special events for my return, and pulled all the old files out for perusal early one morning after Lisa had left, but found my mind wandering to thoughts of Toddy's letters to Granny. Would they provide a key to help unlock the mystery of his disappearance? If so, how could I track them down?

Mum arrived with sandwiches and a vanilla slice. She knew how to win my heart.

'Letters?' she mulled, after my tentative inquiry regarding Toddy, wondering if he may have written to Granny with some story ideas.

'Yes he wrote,' good old Mum.

'So where do you think the letters might be?' I coaxed.

'Who knows? I don't have a clue, Donovan, but you could start by checking the old locked bureau in the attic. The key's on your keyring.'

Simple!

Since moving into Granny's cottage, I hadn't overcome the feeling that it was hers and still respected her privacy. The keyring had many keys of all different shapes and sizes, but the only one I had ever used was the front door key.

Up in the cobwebbed attic, I discovered several old trunks and a small chest of drawers which must have been made by great, great granddad. It was small and beautifully made with ornate 19th century detail and butterfly motifs on each corner.

The bureau was also small, knee-high to me. It had a shelf deep enough for good-sized books, with a let-down desk which was locked. The keyhole required a small key, which narrowed my choice to four on the keyring, so finding the right one wasn't as complicated as I expected.

With some trepidation, I unlocked the desk and found inside several bundles of letters tied with coloured silk ribbons. There was also a colour decoder taped to the desk which helped place the letters in some order, and I soon discovered it was not a chronological order, but that granny had arranged them according to content: Bassenthwaite Lake, Cotehill woods, Michael Scott, Long Meg, Allonby, Poppy and many more.

I delayed reading them until Lisa returned later that day. Together we extracted what we thought were the most significant from each bundle, and realised that Conan's quest involved much more than finding Toddy.

Chapter 12

The Letters

June 3rd
The Brig
Keswick

Dear Indigo,
As promised, I'm sending you an update. Since I first wrote things have evolved significantly. I've been to the Lakeside every day, but still no sightings. Maybe Conan got it wrong. How are things with you? I hope the children are well. Have you seen Poppy again? I'll be at the Brig for a week longer, then move on to Yorkshire for a week. The stories are going down very well. Conan's collection is popular.
Your dear friend, Tim.

June 8th

Dear Indigo,
Thanks for your swift response and the message from Poppy. I'll look into that today after the session. If what she says is true, it will change things considerably, and I may have to stay another day. I went to the Lake last night and there was some activity. I think the troupe has returned. Next week I'll be in Yorkshire, then back to Allonby. I'll write to you from there. Enjoy the summer days in the Wood.
Your friend, Tim.

June 23rd
Allonby,

Dear Indigo,
It's wonderful to be back here by the seaside. Your letter was waiting for me and your mention of Michael Scott is worrying. I'll be in Penrith next week and will visit Long Meg while there. Meanwhile try not to worry, I'll see you at Cotehill soon.
Your great friend, Tim.

July 2

Dear Indigo,
I've been in Keswick for two days now at the storytellers' convention. I met a few old friends. Harold Harper and Jake Dinksworth were there and send their best wishes. These conventions are like heaven for me and they set me up with inspiration and ideas for the year ahead. We have a few southerners who've brought stories of the Piskies and Bogworts with them. I remember Conan mentioning them once or twice and think I'll visit Cornwall one day to get a few ideas. They might like to hear a few tales of mine. I went to visit Long Meg and her Daughters, and was as intrigued as ever. I managed to speak to Meg at sundown. Don't worry I think all is well. She wants me to return tomorrow evening as she has another message for me. After the conference I've decided to travel to Cornwall with Sidney Snoper, one of the storytellers from the south, so won't be back in your neck of the woods for a while. I hope you're all well and promise to return for the autumn.
Your great friend, Tim.

Lisa and I poured over all the letters, twenty five in total, and decided that those four were the most significant regarding clues. However, they didn't make the quest any easier. What's all this about Long Meg and a message? Who was Michael Scott? Did Toddy go to Cornwall and more importantly, did he return to Cotehill by the autumn? The questions were becoming too many, and the answers too few.

It was mid-November and I'd returned to college. Simon had a Wednesday gig planned for the Blue Moon and life seemed to be returning to normal. Conan hadn't visited for a while and I had essays to write for the college course, but Lisa and I tried to keep a thread of the quest alive.

'Michael Scott was a mathematician and scholar in the Middle Ages. He was born somewhere in the border regions of Scotland or northern England.' Lisa was reading from the encyclopaedia she'd brought from home.

'Sounds like an interesting character,' I mulled, blowing on a toasted marshmallow. We were having a cosy evening in the cottage, while the wind howled outside.

'Yes but Don, listen to this... He is said to have turned to stone a coven of witches, which are thought to be entrapped in a stone circle now known as Long Meg and Her Daughters.'

'Lisa! You're amazing! This is significant. Toddy mentions Scott in his letters to Granny, and Long Meg keeps cropping up. There's a definite connection somewhere. He seems to be some sort of medieval wizard, but what can he have to do with Toddy in the 20th century. And where's Conan? He must have some answers, but he never sticks around long enough.'

My frustration began to get the better of me and I dropped the marshmallow leaving a sticky goo on the rug when I tried to clean it.

'He's also famous for discovering something about rainbows,' Lisa continued.

'Anything to do with finding a pot of gold at the end of one?'

'It's happened more often than you'd imagine, Don boy.' The voice was now familiar to me, but Lisa jumped out of her chair and squealed as if she'd seen a ghost. I reassured her that all was well and introduced Conan, who was perched on the mantelpiece beside my Great, Great Granddad Seth's picture. He looked more raggedy than ever; his hair was matted and his clothes appeared to be caked in mud. I supposed the winter could be rough on brownies who had to furrow and burrow through the muddy earth. Poppy appeared, out of the blue, tiny and radiant, in her bright red frock. Lisa was still in shock and speechless.

'Hello Lisa,' Conan chirped. 'I'm that odd friend of Don's he keeps mentioning, and this is fairy Poppy. Happy to meet you young lady. You are very intelligent.' It struck me then how kind and good natured he was; a very likeable character.

'Hello, Lisa, you're doing a fine job helping our Don.' Poppy smiled. She twinkled, just like the fairies in story books. Lisa recovered from the shock; after all in some ways I had prepared her for this eventuality, although up until now she had clung to an element of disbelief. The proof now stared her in the face.

Conan and Poppy stayed until midnight talking and answering a few of our questions although they had a habit of skirting round the question so as to leave you wondering what on earth the answer was, and sometimes there was a glint of mischief in their eyes and they'd exchange glances, as if to say; *They'll never work it out*.

'Conan,' I ventured, 'why do you want us to find Timothy?' A glance exchanged. 'What have Long Meg and her daughters got to do with Timothy's disappearance?' Another exchange. 'Is Michael Scott involved in any way?' Raised eyebrows, but no answer.

'We can't tell you, Don, it's important that you work it out for yourself. All to do with a mild spell, you see.'

'A mild spell?' I repeated. He said it as if he was referring to a mild head cold.

'Yes, nothing too serious, but you're the chosen one in the breaking it department.' This was getting ridiculous. How on this earth could I be involved in the breaking of a spell I knew nothing about.

'Why ME?' I asked annoyed and perplexed.

'Why not you, Don? You have a distant affiliation with Timothy. You're both storytellers who knew your granny. You both play the tin whistle and wear top hats. You're the obvious choice and, I should mention, there's a time limit on this and failure could mean dire consequences.'

'Oh really?' I retorted, feeling unwilling to pursue the whole thing any further, now that a threat was involved.

Poppy pushed Conan to one side. 'Donovan, don't be alarmed. It's just Conan's little way, sometimes he gets a bit threatening, but nothing to worry about. However, the search for Timothy could do with being stepped up a notch, and you do happen to be the only one to break the spell.

Lisa was silent and looked worried, I was fuming. Poppy continued while Conan stood by, miffed.

'And how exactly do I step up the search? Perhaps the police should be informed?' I went to pick up the phone. 'It's not a police matter, Don. It's Fairy.' Poppy explained patiently.

And they both disappeared.

Lisa made a cup of tea and attached a couple of marshmallows to forks in an attempt to return to normality, but both of us were frantically racking our brains to work out what was going on, and what we should do next.

Chapter 13

Captured in Stone

Sunday found us standing in the rain at a very windy Long Meg's stone circle at Little Selkeld near Penrith. We rode there on Ivanhoe, then parked up and walked for a while against the wind, with raindrops pounding our cheeks and seeping through our waterproofs.

The circle is an astounding bronze age construction; fifty nine stones measuring a hundred metres on its axis. Long Meg is made of sandstone and stands twelve feet high.

Lisa had brought a few notes she'd jotted down and, struggling to stay upright in the now blizzard-like wind, tried to read them. Finally, we sheltered behind the big stone, Meg.

'If you count the stones twice and get the same number Michael Scott's spell will be broken and it will bring bad luck; also Meg is thought to have been a 17th century witch called Meg of Meldon.'

We walked from one stone to the next, twenty seven of them are upright and it must be said that the tall one, Meg, looks convincingly witch-like from a certain angle. What could it have to do with Toddy? I mused. Could he also have been turned to stone? Is he here, trapped and somehow watching us and waiting for me to break the spell and release him? It seemed unbearable to contemplate. If it were the truth, Tim was leading this nightmarish existence. I thought about him with Granny and the warm friendship they shared, and his kindly letters as he travelled the country entertaining people and leaving them with good memories. What a dreadful fate this was for such a colourful character, and Conan was right; I did have an affiliation to him and suddenly felt it my duty to help in some way, but here there were no clues, only a miserably cold, wet, bleak landscape full of mystery and ancient deeds.

'Let's go,' I said, and we trudged back to Ivanhoe, who battled the elements to take us home to Cotehill and the cottage in the wood where we piled logs on the fire and warmed up with cups of hot chocolate.

Chapter 14

Revelations

The image of the stones and the thought of Toddy being trapped there haunted me for days. I anguished over what to do. Should I speak to the Bishop and ask about lifting curses and could he possibly do it for an old storyteller who disappeared years ago? However, I knew he'd think I was out of my mind.

I was so distracted I couldn't work on the Shakespeare essay I had to hand in on Wednesday, and no matter how much I tried, *A Midsummer Night's Dream*, would swiftly drift into a midwinter day's nightmare, and Long Meg would loom in my imagination where Puck should have been.

I decided to visit Mum and Dad in the village and escape the torment of my mind, although my mind came with me, of course.

'Have you ever heard of a man called Michael Scott? 'I asked Mum as she peeled potatoes to mash and have with sausages.

'Michael Scott?' she mulled.

'Yes, he was a sort of medieval wizard, like Gandalf, an alchemist.'

'Hmm, I don't know about that one, but we had a Michael Scott in the village some time ago. He was a friend of your granny's. One of the regular visitors to the house. He played the banjo.'

'WHAT?'

'Something happened to him. Let me think. I seem to recall he developed pneumonia and passed away, quite young. We were all very sad about it.'

'In his letters to Granny, Toddy Oggy mentions him and says something to do with him was very worrying.'

'Yes that was probably his sickness. It lasted a few weeks before he passed away. We were all worried.'

'Toddy also mentions going to see Long Meg and her Daughters to talk to them.' Mum laughed.

'Ohh yes! Long Meg and her Daughters was the nickname Toddy and Granny gave to Toddy's sister Meg and his nieces. She was tall like him and it was their little joke.'

I hardly tasted the bangers and mash, as images of Lisa and me at the rain sodden stone circle, freezing and soaking wet, imagining Timothy Ogden entrapped in one of the stones, loomed vivid in my mind. How was I going to break this news to Lisa and avoid her everlasting wrath?

It was hard to adjust my perception of events, from Toddy being trapped inside a stone, to him not being trapped inside a stone. From Michael Scott the wizard, being involved in Toddy's disappearance, to his non-involvement. After all the research and the long journey to Little Selkeld. Nothing was of any significance. I phoned Lisa with the news. She was silent for a few moments, then hung up on me. I couldn't blame her.

Sitting down at my tiny desk, I pulled the essay out for another attempt, only to find it was finished. Five hundred beautifully scripted words on the significance of Puck's character in a *Midsummer Night's Dream*.

'My favourite play,' said an invisible Conan, obviously too shamefaced to put in an appearance after leading Lisa and me astray when he and Poppy could have warned us not to follow that particular trail.

I went to bed.

Chapter 15

A Spell

Cotehill wood, 1950.

Silvery moon shine
Inky dark lake
Silence, a small drop
Our sweet spell will make
Tinkers and tailors
Old witch's brooms
Timothy Ogden
Indigo Dunes
Tails of the forest
Tales of the land
Tales from the old times
Will walk hand in hand
Gather them precious
Gather them gold
Tell them, the treasures
Lest lost in the mist
Timothy Ogden
Indigo Dunes
Our spell will expire
Twentyfold new moons
The earth then in strife
Young blood must find
Moonshine and sunset
Dew drops from dawn
Tender new snowdrops

Our new spell is born.

Chapter 16

Bassenthwaite

The essay was well received at college and the Blue Moon gig that evening went down exceptionally well. Afterwards, Simon introduced me to the manager of a small theatre company that toured the country. He wanted to know if I'd be interested in joining them on a trial basis. He was passionate about the traditional heritage of my stories, and believed they should be preserved. He was also a Friend of the Earth, and wanted his company to promote anything to do with preserving the planet. What could I say? This was an invitation to follow my dream.

    I'd joined the Friends of the Earth while at school and been quite active for a while. At that time the damage to the ozone layer was becoming clear, so I stopped using aerosol deodorant and switched to roll-on. Most people thought I was over-reacting, but I'd seen the diagrams and read the literature. Some other issues back then were nuclear power and recycling glass bottles. It was early days for planet saving and I felt I was doing my bit, so teaming up with the Thistle Theatre Group was perfect.

    Simon was really making up for his cruel comment back in August, but deep down I couldn't help but suspect that Conan had a hand in all the good luck coming my way, and he felt very bad about the incident with Long Meg. Hence a double dose of luck.

    The weeks developed a pattern of lectures, study, the Blue Moon on Wednesdays and Theatre group on Sundays. Sometimes I was the stand-alone storyteller, and sometimes they produced a drama, inspired by my story. Dave was pleased with the way things were going and we had a few excellent write ups in the *Cumberland News*.

Lisa came round after the Long Meg incident, and although we were both busy, we knew we must continue the hunt for Timothy/Toddy, since there was a spell involved, and as I was implicated in the spell, it seemed sensible to delve further.

We read all of the letters again in case we'd missed something.

'Now that Long Meg's off the scene, we still have Bassenthwaite Lake, Keswick, Allonby and Cornwall to consider.' Lisa read the list from her note pad, which was a bit dog eared as it was the same one she'd used at Little Selkeld in the wind and rain.

'We've done Allonby,' I offered.' You can tick it off.'

'I'm not too sure we have, Don. Let's leave it on for now, but I think the next trip should be to Bassenthwaite Lake.'

'It seems that there's a fairy castle just off the main A66, near to the lake. And Elva Hill is believed to be a fairy hill where there's a gateway to a secret world.'

I'd found these gems of information in one of Granny's books about the Lake District and someone - probably Granny - had underlined the words, so I didn't have to work too hard to find them.

'A fairy castle sounds promising,' Lisa replied. 'Don! Here we are seriously considering visiting a fairy castle as if we were planning to visit Big Ben in London.' We had to laugh at the absurdity of it.

Lisa took a day off from the library on Saturday and we caught the bus to Bassenthwaite village. It was now early December, and there was snow on the mountain tops and the sky was clear blue. I recall the peace more than anything. We sat on the grass a while and watched. The lake was still and reflected the surrounding trees.

Lisa pulled out a map on which she had marked the place where the fairy castle stood. 'This way' she announced, pulling me up.

It was where we expected it to be and certainly could have been a fairy castle from its appearance, which comprised of a rocky outcrop in a grassy knoll. The top was covered in grass, but beneath was what appeared to be and, if the legend was to be believed, in fact was, the gateway to fairyland. We stared at it for a while, then I got down on my knees and peered in, but saw only soil, roots, grass and a few hardy wild flowers. I was perplexed.

Lisa knelt down beside me and peered in also, then before our eyes a miniscule piece of paper poked through the soil as if being pushed from the inside. We expected to see a badger emerge, but only the paper arrived. Lisa picked it up, and I immediately recognised it as resembling the first note I had from Conan. It glowed and the handwriting was perfectly formed.

> *Thank you for being a friend of our Earth.*
> *Good luck with your quest for Toddy.*
> *We will help if we can.*

We read the note together as it glowed violet and gold and then was gone. Between my fingers I held nothing.

We hardly spoke a word all the way home on the bus, both deep in our own thoughts. We hadn't really expected to see or find anything at the fairy castle, and what we did find was truly amazing and beautiful. If only you could see how those notes glow and the delicate tiny script. You would never forget the sight.

From the top deck, I watched the wintry beauty of Cumbria; rolling hills strewn with woolly sheep and watchful cows, a landscape of farms and mountains, stunning to behold. I thought about my first encounter with Conan and the strange turn my life had taken; chats with fairies and brownies, a spell in which I was ensnared and which I must somehow find Timothy Ogden in order to escape the consequences, and now a good luck message from the fairy castle, but no clue regarding the quest for Toddy.

'This has to be a dream,' I said as we arrived at Carlisle Bus Station.

'I don't think it is Don. I've been trying to wake up all the way home,' said Lisa as we crossed the road for hot chocolate at Watts, before catching the bus to Cotehill, whereIvanhoe was waiting at Mum and Dad's house.

'Bassenthwaite Lake? How lovely, Donovan. Beautiful at

this time of year, in spite of the cold. Any particular reason for going?' Mum was dishing up a large bowl of hearty chicken soup. Just what was needed on a cold December night.

'We went to find the fairy castle.' Mum hesitated for a nano-second as she ladled the soup. An almost imperceivable standstill of her whole being, but I saw it; a reaction, not just of surprise, but something deeper and more meaningful. It told me she knew. It told me that all along she had known.

'Oh indeed? The fairy castle. Granny told us so many stories about the fairy castle and its inhabitants. She had such a great imagination.' She was bluffing.

'Except it wasn't imagination was it, Mum? Did you ever meet Conan?'

'Conan!' She was startled and looked at me with disbelief.' Then Dad came home.

'Donovan, Son! Good to see you. How go the stories? Ready to give up yet and join your dad making heaps of dosh? That soup smells good Emily.'

Dad continued rattling on about the factory and new investors and expansion and turn-over and money. I stopped listening and could only wonder about what Mum knew. How did she know? I had so many questions, but it wouldn't be wise to bring up the subject in Dad's presence. I was almost certain Mum wouldn't have shared stories about fairies and brownies with him.

After tea, I left them watching a TV game show and returned to the cottage. To my relief, Simon and the gang were waiting in the garden ready to build a bonfire. I needed some light relief. Life was becoming too complicated and extremely weird.

Chapter 17

Wrapped in Plastic

Something snapped that day. It was all too much to comprehend, and the thought of Mum being entangled in the tale was decidedly strange. I entered a phase of denial, much to Lisa's annoyance: 'You can't give up, Don. The fairies are depending on us. And what about Toddy?' I told her I'd stopped caring and wanted to lead a normal life from now on. 'That's impossible! There's no turning back,' she said dramatically. But my mind was made up. I went along to the theatre group gig at Whitehaven on Sunday, but had no enthusiasm. Simon was there and I told him I was quitting and that I'd honour the gigs he'd planned but not to make any more bookings. It transpired he'd booked me through until January, and the Blue Moon was a fixture. I agreed to continue for a while, but my heart was no longer in it. Simon and Dave tried to reason with me. They were perplexed, and I couldn't tell them the reason for my quitting. Imagine their faces if I said I was under a spell and needed to find Toddy Oggy in order to break it, and I'd had a note from the fairies at the fairy castle at Bassenthwaite, and that I had regular visits from a brownie called Conan and a fairy called Poppy. I felt sad, but knew I was doing the right thing.

That evening Conan appeared as I was watching *Whistle Test* and a really cool Jonny Winter concert. I ignored him and he said nothing. He stayed for around an hour while Winter played his guitar, and each time I looked at him he became fainter and fainter until he disappeared completely. I must admit to feeling deeply saddened, but needed to be strong and clear the situation from my life.

Over the next few weeks I refused to discuss the fairies with Lisa, who at first, was determined to continue. Eventually she stopped trying to engage me and in fact stopped speaking to me. After the January gigs I gave up storytelling and left the theatre group. I had plenty of college work piling up to keep me busy, and decided to become a model student, attend all the lectures and stay on top of the work.

Dad was overjoyed at my transformation, especially when I got a haircut.

Looking back it was obvious I was trying to fit in. I had rejected all the odd stuff because I could no longer cope with it and also the quest for Toddy was wrecking my life and my future.

The extra work paid off and I graduated with a good degree. Now and then I'd see Lisa around Carlisle and college, but eventually she slipped away. Don't get me wrong, it hurt badly, but I had to shut all the fairy stuff out of my life.

I began work at the factory, where Dad gave me an office and responsibility for the TV meal packaging. People were just getting into convenience food at that time and it hadn't quite taken off, but demand was increasing and I became engrossed in numbers. We were trying to develop the market at home and abroad, so I had to travel a lot around the country and beyond, with our samples of packaging. The business was really taking off, and we were making a pile of money. Ivanhoe became redundant when I bought my first car - a BMW - which I would proudly drive through the village. Once I passed Lisa on her bike and waved. She didn't wave back.

I began to think about changing the cottage in some way; adding an extension, perhaps building up to have an extra floor or out to extend the ground space, or both even. Dad suggested I sell it and buy a house in the village or Carlisle, but I wasn't ready to do that yet, although renting was a possibility and good for the bank balance. Also, if I moved out, I could erase all the memories of Conan and Poppy and storytelling.

The house I found was in Stanwix, a pleasant area of Carlisle close to Bitts Park, where I could walk my dog... when I eventually got one. I kept the cottage for the time being, but life in the town was appealing. There were restaurants, shops and clubs to enjoy spending my money, which was plentiful; I finally understood why Dad had wanted me to join the factory. I was having fun!

Two years went by in a flash; so much was happening at once. The new job, new car, new house and new me I suppose. Talk about no looking back!

I kept in touch with most of my friends and they were impressed... I think. At least they liked to be ferried around in the BMW. Simon hardly spoke to me at first, after all, he'd lost his job and couldn't understand the change that had come over me; I'd buried it all so much in the past now that Conan and Poppy had become like a figment of my imagination. They had no place in my new reality.

Mum never questioned my decisions, but I sensed she had reservations, especially as she was so attached to the cottage.

'I hate to think of the cottage being neglected and deserted,' she told me one day when I was visiting Cotehill, but my heart was hardened.

'I check on it now and again,' I reassured her. 'Everything's fine.'

She was silent. There was something on her mind, but I didn't want to ask her because I was sure it would dredge up the fairy past I had left behind.

My mind was firmly on other things these days. We had a new yogurt carton contract in Denmark, and were chasing one in Amsterdam. Plastic was really taking off, and Dad wanted to expand to make drinks' can holders and plastic bottles. People started to prefer spring water to tap water, and plastic bottles were becoming big business.

I started dating a girl called Steph, whose dad owned a small supermarket chain. We met at one of the packaging conventions in London, and my dad was over the moon about it.

'You've found yourself a gold mine there, Donovan. Our factory and their outlet stores would be a great match. There was a time I thought I'd never say it Son, but I'm proud of you.' He hugged me and I realised he'd never done that before.

Steph was slim, blonde and blue eyed. She was into fast cars and flashy holidays, so I changed my car and bought a little open-topped sports number, and we drove to the South of France, where we met a lot of her friends, who were all jet-setters. Usually I'd visit her in London, but once or twice she stayed with me at my Stanwix house. We'd call at Mum and Dad's house and on the first occasion I remember passing Lisa riding her bike up the long winding hill into Cotehill village, her hair loose to her waist, and she still wore her granny specs. We didn't acknowledge each other.

The second time Steph and I called in on Mum and Dad, there was a wonderful spread waiting for us. Mum had excelled herself; quiche and chips with salad and lemon meringue to follow. She knew my favourites and it was great to have some home-made food for a change. Steph and I frequented a lot of restaurants. Dad opened a bottle of something pricey, and we talked a lot about plastics and supermarkets. As we were leaving, Dad walked us to the gate.

'You know, Steph, I can't tell you how happy I am that Donovan has found you. There was a time I despaired of him ever joining the human race, what with that Conan fellow turning his head and all. He'd tried it on me, when I was a whipper-snapper, but I'd have nothing to do with him.' He laughed and shook his head to emphasise his point. Silence ensued as Mum and I exchanged shocked glances.

'Who's Conan?' asked Steph. 'He sounds like a bad guy.'

Chapter 18

Back to the Wood

Later that day I waved Steph off at the train station and drove straight the my cottage. It was late October and I hadn't been there since July, when I called to pick up a few things for my new house.

I couldn't stop thinking about Dad's words to Steph about Conan. The idea that my Dad, and probably Mum, had met Conan was more disturbing that actually meeting Conan. There was something sinister in the secrecy.

As I parked the car next to Ivanhoe, a deep sadness gripped me. My trusty steed was rusting beneath a tangle of Russian vine; forlorn and neglected. I recalled the good times of speeding through the woods all weathers, and the earthy smell of wild flowers and rain soaked peat. My heart ached as I lingered by the fire pit where the gang had gathered and Conan first appeared. Inside, Granny's tiny furniture was dusty and cobwebbed. My top hat lay on the dresser beside Great, Granddad Seth's picture. Two years had passed since I turned my back on it all. 'Why did I do that?'

I had never questioned it. Something had snapped the day we went to Bassenthwaite Lake and I suspected Mum knew about Conan. It had all become overwhelming; but why take the path I had? Why did I jump into a life I'd rejected so vehemently and embrace it full throttle, pushing Lisa away and dumping Ivanhoe? It was as if I was under a spell, like the boy Kai in Hans Anderson's *Snow Queen*, with a glass splinter in his eye, I had become brittle.

I sat in the big chair, deep in thought until the sun set and darkness fell, wondering what had removed the glass splinter from my eye, and realised it was the moment my Dad mentioned Conan's name. It was as if the thin veil of illusion lifted and I stood at their garden gate feeling like I'd just been placed there from nowhere and my clothes, the car, Steph, my job belonged to another person who existed pre-Dad's comment, but was no more.

I was back.

It felt wonderful to be me again, but I had a life that no longer belonged to me, and an old life that also no longer belonged to me. I was in-between.

'Welcome back, Don, boy!' It was Conan, perched on the little stool beside me. It felt like a reunion with one of my oldest friends and that evening, for the first time in two years, he and I talked for a long time, and I slept in my old room again, listening to the owls as I nodded off.

The next morning I called in sick and spent the day at my cottage dusting and polishing, gathering wood for the stove and tidying the garden. Ivanhoe needed a lot of attention, so I drove to Halfords for a few parts and a can of oil, and to the village shop to stock up on food, then spent the afternoon fixing my bike. By the end of the day I had recovered a small fraction of my life and felt better for it, but there was much to be done. Conan was only able to verify that Lisa and I had been on the right track until my derailment and that somehow Dad had reached the same point in his youth, but hadn't found his way back. He'd also hinted at a few more clues and suggested I contact Simon as soon as possible. All was not lost, but I knew I had to have a long talk with Mum and Dad, so invited them to tea in the woods.

They declined.

My parents left the country that week to holiday in Spain for a month. I was to take care of the business. I hadn't had time to tell them of my return to me, and looking after a plastic factory was a bit risky, but I wasn't quite ready to burn the place down.

Steph was perplexed at the change. I decided to come clean and tell her the whole truth over the phone.

'Steph, there's something I need to tell you. Two years ago I changed; remember my dad mentioned it? I wasn't interested in the factory or the business, and I used to travel round telling stories; also I was a Friend of the Earth.'

'A what?' Steph interrupted.

'A Friend of the Earth. Someone who cares about what happens to our planet, and tries to do something about pollution and stuff like that.'

Silence.

'So one day a brownie called Conan visited me and set me a quest to find a lost storyteller called Toddy Oggy, or Timothy Ogden as some may know him.'

Silence.

'Then, my then girlfriend Lisa and I went in search of him, first to Long Meg's, and then to the fairy castle at Bassenthwaite, because a fairy called Poppy suggested that might help, but all they told us was to keep searching and wished us luck.'

Steph hung up.

She never contacted me again.

I wasn't surprised.

Chapter 19

Finding Donovan

As part of my reconstruction project, I phoned Simon to let him know I was back in action. He was a bit cool, but said he'd contact the Blue Moon and Dave, although after two years, things had moved on, so I may need to audition and come up with something impressive if they were to consider me again. I dug out the tin whistle and played a few tunes for the first time since my exit from the story scene.

I was now dividing my time between the house in Stanwix and the cottage. Ivanhoe was back in action, and I only used the car for long journeys. I also re-joined Friends of the Earth. Life was almost back to normal, and my hair had almost reach my shoulders, but there was a vacuum that seemed impossible to fill, even though I longed to. Lisa was still living in the village and still had a job at the library. I often saw her cycling up the hill at the end of the day, and noticed a slight reaction when I passed her on Ivanhoe one December twilight as the sun was setting behind us; a huge red ball of fire casting a pink glow across the fields.

On the Saturday before Christmas, my parents were still out of the country. The factory seemed to be getting along without me; there were plenty of managers and sub-managers to keep things going, so I stayed home to work on a few stories. The Blue Moon had agreed to have me back for a night on Wednesday. I woke early for a stroll through the woods. How could I have turned my back on this? There was a mild frost which blanched the fir trees and they glistened in the sunlight. Frozen bracken lined the path and the frosted grass crunched underfoot.

I wandered for an hour, then returned to the cottage, planning to toast some crumpets for breakfast. It was so cold I could see my breath, and when I reached the cottage there was Lisa, muffled in a red woolly hat and scarf, waiting as if she had never left. My heart was full.

'So you're back,' she said.

'Yes I'm back,' I replied.

Inside, we quietly prepared breakfast, then sat at the table. The silence lasted until the crumpets were consumed. We knew there was a lot to say, but where to begin was the problem. Trivialities seemed inadequate.

'I don't know why I did it,' was the most meaningful statement I could muster.

'It had something to do with the spell,' Lisa replied. 'Poppy warned me and said you'd eventually come round, but it could be years and years. I suppose two years isn't bad when you think about it.'

We were back in business.

For hours we talked about our lives since the glitch, as we called it. Lisa knew most of what I'd been up to. It seemed I'd been the talk of the village with my flash car and girlfriend. Meanwhile, Lisa had taken over Mrs. Frith's job at the library and was now in charge. She was also a Friend of the Earth and had taken to fell walking around the Lake District.

'What do you think brought you back, Don?' she asked.

'It had something to do with my dad; he knew Conan, and as soon as he revealed the fact, it was as if a spell lifted. I was me again.'

'Poppy said it would only be a matter of time. It seems your dad has been in denial about his encounters with Conan, hence he's been sucked into the phony world of plastic, just as you were. But you managed to escape. Remember when Conan said that whenever you concentrated on finding Timothy Ogden, life would pick up a notch? You had a lot of success with the storytelling in those days.'

The fire was almost out. There was much to think about, but Lisa had to leave. I walked her to the village, pushing her bike, and we arranged to meet the next day, which was Sunday. I noticed the light was on in my parents' house and their car parked in the drive; they were back from their travels but I wasn't ready to talk to them yet. Lisa and I kissed good night at her gate, and I returned to the woods where the unexpected and inexplicable was about to happen.

Chapter 20

The Fairy Line

It was pitch dark along the path home, but I had a torch with me. Being so familiar with the terrain, the darkness didn't faze me and soon the clouds cleared and a bright moon lit my path. Then, ahead of me I noticed a line of lights low on the ground. It extended a long way into the woods and I couldn't fathom what it was, although my first thought was that a colony of ants was busy at work. However, I'd never known ants to glow. Upon reaching the start of the line I realised I was witnessing a fairy event. They didn't acknowledge my presence, if they were in fact aware of it. They were passing objects along from one to another, and when the object reached the end of the line it disappeared. Kneeling down for a closer look I saw plastic bottle tops, plastic bottles, plastic bags, plastic yogurt cartons, all being passed along the line from one to another. I followed the line deep into the wood until I reached the beginning, where the objects seemed to appear from nowhere.

'They're cleaning up the mess, Don.' Conan had appeared beside me and was watching.

'Where's it coming from?' I asked, as there was no visible source.

'Everywhere, it's coming from everywhere; the oceans, the rivers, lakes, parks, its choking up the planet and humans aren't doing enough. We fairies are working on it, but the problem's growing. You've seen inside the factory, the plans for more and more plastic. It won't decompose, Don and there'll be more and more of it.'

We watched the fairies at work. Patiently dealing with

the mess humans were creating. There was no jolly singing and dancing. It was a solemn line and I felt deep shame and anger as I walked away.

'Did you know that at first plastic was hailed as the saviour of wild animals and the human race? Seems it replaced ivory to make golf balls, therefore saving the lives of hundreds of elephants.' Lisa had phoned late one evening, as I was planning my story session. I'd told her about the fairy clean up gang and she was so upset that she'd decided to research the plastic phenomena, in the hope that if we understood it better we would be in a better position to help the fairies.

'Unbelievable!' I responded. 'Funny how things can change.' Of course there wasn't much I didn't know about the stuff, but had to admit to ignorance as regards its history. From the hero material of the day, plastic was slowly becoming the enemy of the planet, and yet it wasn't going to go away, no matter how long the fairies worked at it. A more creative solution was needed.

'Any new ideas for finding Toddy?' I ventured.

'I think your parents may be able to help us with that, Don. Your mum knew him, and if your dad had dealings with Conan, I'm guessing he also knew Toddy. Do you think Michael Scott's death is somehow part of the jigsaw?'

'An interesting thought, Lisa. One that hadn't crossed my mind, but let's explore it some time.'

Mum called round while I was in residence at my Stanwix house. She'd been shopping in town and breezed in with a bunch of flowers and a cherry pie.

'Put the kettle on, Donovan. I can't stay long; just called to say hello and see how you are.' After I'd asked a few questions about their holiday, I dove straight in and asked her how Dad knew Conan; she hesitated and I thought she was about to leave, but then she talked.

Chapter 21

Dark Secrets

'As you know Donovan, I had the most amazing childhood at the cottage, and yes Conan was a frequent visitor, as was fairy Poppy and many other fairies. The Bassenthwaite troupe I mentioned, often travelled to Cotehill wood from Bassenthwaite castle, and we'd have evenings of singing and dancing, literally magic times. It was all very secret of course, if people knew there were fairies in Cotehill wood, they'd come in their droves to look for them. Toddy and Mike Scott were there a lot, also. Toddy was a great storyteller, who travelled the country to find his tales. He'd go to Ireland, Cornwall, Lancashire and all over the place, to find a good story and wherever he went, the fairy folk helped him find the best and oldest of stories.'

Mum sipped her tea, but her thoughts were far away from my kitchen.

'I was privileged to have Indigo for my mum and to be part of the beautiful world of fairy, for it was beautiful; they twinkled and glowed and made everything around them glow such bright, vivid colours. They brightened the woods in the deepest, darkest night, flitting about like fireflies.'

'So what happened to change it all, Mum?' I asked, certain it must have been something bad.

'I met your Dad,' she answered flatly. I was sixteen and he was seventeen and worked at the petrol station in the village, but always had ambitions to open a factory, and also had a fascination for plastic. He'd made some at school once in a chemistry lesson and said he saw all the possible use it could be put to. Anyway he asked me out, and we started dating.

Before long, I knew he was the one for me and took him home to meet Indigo. Of course Toddy was there that day and Mike Scott. To cut a very long story short, Conan asked your dad to do something. He wanted him to find a storyteller somewhere in Ireland. Said only that man knew how to break the spell.'

'What spell,?' I interrupted.

'We never found out. Your dad flatly refused and said he wanted no more to do with any of them. He asked me to marry him and made me promise never to speak to Conan and the fairies again. Soon after that he started his little factory. And the rest is history, as they say. As a result of all this, Toddy ended up being the one to search for the storyteller. The last time Granny heard from him, I think he was in Keswick and planned to go to Cornwall, but his ultimate destination was Ireland, although we never heard from him again and while he was away, Michael Scott was complaining of sleepless nights when he'd be riding horse back in his dreams and wake up in a sweat. He became ill and couldn't eat; talked all the time about a black horse speeding and about a grey landscape. The doctors thought he had pneumonia at first, but some disagreed, truth is they didn't know what it was and he died.'

'Mum, that sounds like what I was in hospital with, and I also had a similar dream the night before Lisa found me. I was riding a black horse and it was steaming from the nostrils, it was going so fast.'

There was a long silence, while we contemplated the strangeness of it. Neither of us asked the question, but it lay there between us. Does that mean I'm going to die?

'One more thing, Donovan. When your dad said he didn't want anything to do with Conan and the fairies, one of the bad fairies - they do exist - put a spell on him out of anger. I was there when she did it. We were all gathered in Granny's living room, and Toddy had been telling some great old stories from the Border Lands. Then it happened. Dad told Conan where to get off and the bad fairy, bursting with fury, flew round and round him saying something in fairy language. Later Indigo said it was a spell which could only be lifted if your dad spoke Conan's name again, and he didn't do that until the day he did, which was the day Steph came to our house.'

'I know that, Mum,' I said. 'I felt it happen. That's why I've reverted to old me. I was ensnared in the spell also, and I think it's because I became aware of your knowledge of Conan's existence. The day I was at your house and you'd made chicken soup, something then told me you knew Conan, and from that moment I lost all interest in the quest for Toddy Oggy, and in my whole life as it was.'

Mum nodded. 'Yes, I thought that's what had happened, but you seemed so much happier in the new life, just like your dad; new house, fast car, beautiful girlfriend, fancy holidays.'

'Mum those things don't make people happy. They disguise unhappiness. The more you get, the more you want and you're sucked into other people's expectations of you. It's a horrible world. Dad's lucky he has you. It could have been so much worse for him, because money attracts the wrong sort of people and you're not that sort,' I said in all sincerity. Mum was the most caring and humble person I knew, apart from Lisa. She was never really part of Dad's rich boastfulness; always kept her distance when he was cracking on about the factory and how rich he was.

'You know why that is, don't you Donovan?' she said. 'It's because I knew about the spell. He wasn't that sort of person before the bad fairy threw that at him. He had ambition, but not greed, and don't forget; the day he mentioned Conan's name, he too was released from the spell.'

I hadn't thought of that. In fact I hadn't seen Dad since that day.

'You may be surprised when you see him. He's changed.' Mum smiled.

Chapter 22

The Plastic Dragon

That Wednesday at the Blue Moon, I included my first planet saving story, influenced by the fairy chain I'd witnessed in the woods:

Once upon a time there was a fire breathing dragon that wanted to destroy planet Earth, and many of Earth's creatures. People thought the dragon's fire was splendid and found a way to recreate it in great palaces devoted to enhancing the power of the dragon. An army of knights were helpless against the dragon's fire which appeared in tiny sparks in every household in all the kingdoms of the planet. The people of the planet were ignorant of the invisible power of the dragon until the day came when the oceans, rivers and lakes were blemished by the dragon's smoky breath, and fish floated dead on their surfaces, poisoned by tiny particles of dragon poison.

The kings in the palaces gained great riches as the power of the dragon spread through every kingdom, and the people in their ignorance enjoyed the sinister presence which disguised itself in myriad of ways.

Only the fairy folk knew how planet Earth was suffering, and worked night and day to extinguish the miniscule sparks of dragon fire. Chains of fairy folk in every ancient wood on planet Earth, glowing in the darkest nights, extracting the dragon poison from the earth, but the poison only grew and the fairy folk became exhausted as their magic lands were afflicted by the breath of the dragon.

* *There seemed to be no way of stopping the progress of its poison and planet Earth began to die, while the kings in the palaces enjoyed the rich rewards bestowed by the dragon to his faithful servants.*

(Here I play a sad tune on the tin whistle.)

Who would kill the dragon and save the planet? He was too strong for the fairy folk and too sly for the people. What could be done? Nobody knew.

The dragon poison spread. There was no way to eliminate it. Great mounds of it appeared and made the streets ugly and the rivers and streams polluted and yet there was nothing to be done.

(sad tune)

Imagine the dragon is plastic. Plastic bags, cartons bottles and all the myriad things we use and then discard.

(show them some items)

These will not disintegrate and the fairy folk can't deal with it. We need to solve the problem before it's too late for Mother Earth.

(stunned silence)

That, my friends, is a fairy tale for our time, but so far there doesn't seem to be a happy ending. Who will kill the plastic dragon?

Then something amazing happened, the room filled with fairies! They appeared in their thousands, filling every nook and cranny, from floor to ceiling, glowing reds, blues, yellows, greens, pinks, indigos, silvers and gold; every colour you can imagine, crowding the room and reciting in unison: 'Kill the plastic dragon! kill the plastic dragon!'

The punters put down their glasses and joined in. Conan flew by me, heartily enjoying himself.

'Good lad, Don! Great story! You got the message across.'

'But, Conan, the fairies secret is out.' I imagined the headlines tomorrow: *Militant Fairies Invade the Blue Moon*. And then the people trying to track them down, an invasion of every woodland from here to Siberia.

'Don't worry, Don boy, they won't remember this. I'll cast a forget-you-ever-saw-it spell, but they will remember your message.' With that they were all gone and the Blue Moon returned to its normal, tavern-like self.

I got a standing ovation, and a few folk stayed behind to talk about their concerns re the planet. Simon was in awe.

'Where did that come from, Don? Great story, and you really grabbed them. I think we're on to a winner! And how do you do that hat thing?' I still hadn't worked out what the hat thing was. For every gig I'd decorate my top hat with some seasonal flowers or items collected in the wood that day, but that was the limit. I did nothing else to the hat.

I suspected Simon's idea of *winning* would be increased bookings and income, but for me, I'd have won if just one person started to save the planet in a small way.

On the way out of the Blue Moon, and to my surprise, I met Dad.

'It's time we talked Donovan,' he said. 'I'll see you at the cottage.'

It felt like a curtain of doom and gloom had descended on a bright, shiny evening. Ivanhoe and I took our time as we enjoyed the crisp February air, and the misty woodland in the moonlight. Dad's Ferrari was parked at the cottage.

I made a cup of tea with jam and muffins. Dad sat in the big chair and I perched on a stool.

'The story, Donovan,' he said.

Here we go. Negativity, negativity. I wanted to cover my ears the way I did as a child, but resisted the temptation.

'Well done! I was very impressed. I've never been so proud of you, Son.'

Yes, you've got it! I fell off the stool, clichéd I know, but that's what happened. It was so unexpected, and good to hear. We both laughed and, for the first time ever, we shared a genuine father – son happy moment. In fact we shared a remarkable few hours, during which Dad apologised for his negativity over the years and said he wanted to join me in the campaign to kill the plastic dragon. I was waiting for him to suggest manufacturing plastic dragons to help the campaign, but luckily, that didn't happen.

We talked about Conan and Toddy, as well as Michael Scott, and he promised to try and help find Toddy.

'I have a few ideas, son. Let's talk about it tomorrow. It's late now.' Sure enough it was two a.m. He drove the short distance home and I waved him off feeling happier that I'd felt in years. I finally had a Dad I could talk to and who was on the same page as me.

Before returning to the cottage, I glanced into the wood and saw the glowing line, as the fairy folk valiantly struggled on to save the planet.

Just as I was nodding off to sleep, Simon phoned; it was now the '80s and some people had a Motorola mobile phone. We called them 'bricks' because of their enormous size, but of course they weren't made of brick, they were made of plastic, in fact, nobody could have predicted the field day the *dragon* was about to have with the rise of technology; computers, games' consoles by the million were about to hit the planet so hard and in such a subtly, sly, sneaky way, through the guise of adding quality to lives, that it was evident there was no way back.

So it was three a.m. and Simon phoned me.

'Don, my phone hasn't stopped ringing since your gig. Newspapers, radio stations, venues. The plastic dragon routine is a hit! I've fixed you up for every evening, starting tomorrow at the Silver Pigeon in Little Selkeld.'

'You mean today?' I answered, sleepily.

'Oh, yes sorry. Today, later.'

The meeting with Dad was shelved until Sunday, when Simon had squeezed in a day off. I called in at his office at the factory, but he wasn't around, so left a message to say I was taking extended leave and would be in touch as soon as possible.

The drive to Little Selkeld in my convertible, was wonderful. There's no better feeling than when you reach the mountain road on the M6 on a sunny day, with the hills either side of you and the winding road ahead, then slip off the motorway and penetrate the countryside. Little Selkeld, you recall, was where the stone circle of Meg and her Daughters stands, and where Lisa and I went in all seriousness in an effort to release Toddy from the stone spell. Lisa was with me for the gig and we laughed about the whole thing and Mum revealing the truth about Toddy's tall sister, Meg.

The Silver Pidgeon stood in a remote position in the midst of a maze of snaking country lanes which would drive a SAT NAV bonkers. Not that we had such things back then, of course. We had a hearty welcome from Jacob, the landlord, and his wife Jill.

'My old mate Jed, Blue Moon Landlord, got in touch last night to recommend you; said you brought the house down. Our Thursday crowd are always up for a good story or two,' he said, generously placing two plates of fish and chips and a pot of tea on the table in front of us.

'Would you like some bread and butter with that love?' Jill asked.

'No thanks this is great! Nice place.' I smiled, glancing around the cosy snug, packed with rural paraphernalia, pictures of pheasants and livestock, cows and bulls, horses and badgers, brass horseshoes and old saddles with willow patterned plates, and old china jugs lining the ancient wooden beams that criss crossed the ceiling. A typical English country Inn.

'We were in these parts a couple of years ago,' I remarked, making conversation. 'Came to see the stones.'

'Ahh old Meg and her Daughters. Fascinating place, especially if you're interested in such things as stone circles and sun alignment, as well as folk lore, of course, and you being a storyteller, it's right up your street or your long and winding road, as you might say,' We all had a laugh about that.

'We were actually here on the trail of an old story-teller called Toddy Oggy, or Timothy Ogden, as some remember him.'

'Toddy! Of course I remember Toddy. Great man and brilliant at this craft. The best storyteller on the planet in my opinion, but I haven't seen your act yet, so I'll tell you later if I've changed my mind. Toddy's niece Gwen will be here tonight, she might be able to tell you something. Last I knew, he was heading for Cornwall, or was it Ireland? Never saw him after that. Must be twenty years or more.'

Lisa and I might well have turned to stone on hearing Jacob's news. It was as if time slammed the breaks on and Jacob's words, 'Toddy's niece will be here later' hung in the air and hovered over our fish and chips, then did a little jig.

'Gwen will be here tonight?' I repeated, as if Gwen was a long lost movie star, I'd spent my life wanting to meet.

'Yes she often pops in. Only lives up the road with her mum, Meg.'

Oh glory! Lisa and I stifled the giggles and ate heartily, feeling our quest may be nearing its end.

The gig went well, with a few old stories from the Scottish Highlands and Glens, then the Plastic Dragon. Even more fairies appeared at the end, if that was possible. Word must have spread to the Bassentwaite troupe at the castle and beyond. Conan re-assured me that the memory eraser spell would be implemented and no fairy habitat would be harmed as a result, but the message would remain.

Afterwards we met Gwen, a softly spoken lady, about my mum's age. She had pale, delicate skin and made me think of lilies in a dewy dawn.

'If you want to know about Toddy, it's my mum you'll need to talk to. I remember him, but didn't really know the person. He was a great storyteller though. Mum will be happy to talk to you. Come on over now; she's a night owl and won't mind one bit.'

Meg was taller than we imagined. Unusually so, maybe six foot eight and mid-sixties, although she didn't look much older than Gwen. When she stood to greet us she towered over us and it was hard to eliminate the image or Long Meg at the stone circle.

'I know,' she smiled, 'I'm very tall, I'll give you a moment to adjust to the shock. Gwen, love put the kettle on. Toddy used to call me Long Meg, although he's taller than me. I'd call him Long Toddy.' We all had a laugh and I was charmed by her warmth.

Once the tea was served and we were all cosy round the fire I explained our quest, missing out the part about Conan and implying that I was interested in meeting her brother, as one story teller to another.

'Wish I could help you dears. I haven't seen Toddy for years, nor heard from him if truth be told. Last time he was here it was late '60s. He had a great night at the Silver Pidgeon and said he had to go to Cornwall and possibly Ireland. He was looking for an old word, no longer in use. Said a friend needed it. I thought he must be losing his grip, what with all the storytelling. I mean most of the time he wasn't living in the real world. So this thing about an old word sounded very plausible for Toddy, but at the same time, a step too far. I asked him what the word was and of course he said he had no idea what it was, that's why he was looking for it.'

A perplexed silence fell and we sipped our tea, contemplating the old word possibilities.

'I wonder if he ever found it?' said Meg eventually.

After a few more niceties it was time for us to leave.

Chapter 23

Craggy Jackson

Lisa and I knew that the old word quest was Conan's doing. Why did he send Toddy off to look for such a silly thing. An old word? What was Conan thinking? And because of it we lost the best storyteller on the planet.

We were at the cottage, it was Sunday and we had the day to spend together. I was polishing Ivanhoe and Lisa was fixing a flat bike tyre. As Simon had implied, my plastic dragon tale was becoming a big thing; I'd already been interviewed by the *Cumberland News* and they'd put a big spread in about the importance of re-cycling and reducing the used of plastic. Some school children had drawn pictures of the dragon and the fairies clearing up the mess he made. I also had a few invitations to visit schools.

'We need that word, Don.' It was Conan. 'It's an old word used in a spell back in the Middle Ages and we've lost it. Without the word we can't break the spell.'

'What spell?' I was harbouring a lot of resentment about Toddy's loss to the storytelling world.

'Follow me, my friends.'

We followed him into the woods. After a while I began to think we were in an unfamiliar part of Cotehill wood, although I prided myself on knowing every tree and where it stood. These trees were unfamiliar and this wood was nothing like the one I knew. Conan trudged on. Eventually we reached an ancient oak tree. Its trunk was as wide as a house and the boughs reached the ground through which poked a thousand fresh green bluebell shoots.

'This tree, Don and Lisa, has stood here for more than

a thousand years. It's at the heart of what you would call fairyland; our core. Long ago a spell was cast to cause the death of this tree after five hundred years. According to our calculations, it has fifty human years left, that's a lot less in fairy years. The only way we can reverse the process is by lifting the spell, and we have some good wizards with the ability to do that. But we've lost a key word. It's a word commonly used back when to spell was cast, but has disappeared from the language. If this tree goes, we go with it, Don. It will mark the end of the Cumbrian branch of the fairy network, no pun intended,'

'But why send Toddy to Cornwall or Ireland?' I asked, still miffed.

'Because those places have storytellers whose stories are almost pure and uncontaminated by modern tradition, stories that have been told through the ages and never written down. Stories with words you've never heard here in Cumbria, with words unspoilt from the day they were first created and put in a story, to be passed through the ages like a gemstone, unspoilt. One of those words, Don and Lisa, is the word we need to save our tree, and indeed our very existence.'

'So, which one first?' I asked. Lisa was studying maps and had a pile of dictionaries beside her on my kitchen table in Stanwix. She was on her lunch break from the library. Of course the Internet wasn't quite up and running yet, although we were beginning to dabble in computers. Books were still king.

'Ireland or Cornwall?'

We chose Cornwall.

'It would be useful to know the context of the lost word,' I suggested to Conan on the eve of our journey to Cornwall. We planned to travel in the convertible, and Simon had booked quite a few gigs along the way. He couldn't come due to work commitments. He was working as the manager of a food factory in Carlisle, and often worked strange shifts, but considering I'd once called him Simon the Insulter, he turned out to be a great manager.

'I can't give you the context, Don. If I did there'd be a danger of the spell perpetrators getting wind that you were on to them and that could be dangerous.'

'Can you narrow the word down to a particular century,

better still decade?' Lisa asked. 'Sixteenth century,' Conan replied, getting impatient.

'Will you be joining us there, Conan?' Lisa asked.

'Wish I could, but I can't leave Cumbria. We have our boundaries,' he answered and disappeared.

We called on my parents to tell them our plans. They were enjoying the early spring sun in the garden. We didn't mention Toddy or the old word scenario. Just kept it to a simple explanation. A few gigs and a short break over the Easter bank holiday.

Mum gave us some sandwiches for the trip and a flask of tea. Dad walked us to the gate and said he had a surprise for me and would tell me about it on my return.

I was intrigued.

We set off on the journey to Cornwall on Friday afternoon and hadgigs at Lancaster, Manchester and Birminghamalong the way, sleeping in the car and taking turns at the wheel. The gigs were well received and attended by the local militant fairies at each venue. Conan had been busy with the grapevine.

The news releases were brilliant and the plastic dragon story was inspiring people up and down the country to make a few changes and be aware of their consumer habits. We reached Cornwall mid-morning on Sunday and headed to Polperro, where I had a booking. It was good to see the incredible coastline and huge waves lashing the rocks. The car was in its element zipping along the coast road, and we soon made it to the bed and breakfast Simon had booked for us.

Polperro was a pretty sight, with its rocky coastland strewn with white houses built onto the cliffs, they looked as if they would topple into the sea with just a little help from the wind.

Our guest house was called The Welcome Inn, a tiny white cottage with a chintzy interior. Once unpacked we headed to the beach for a longed-for dip in the sea. Later we found the venue for that evening; a three story terraced tavern, very narrow along an equally narrow alleyway.

There were pictures of pirates and treasure chests, old sailing ships and the wild waves of the cove. The landlord was Jack, and he introduced us to the resident folk group. I had a few old Cumbrian stories lined up with a King Arthur theme, which interestingly is a common Cornish story theme. Jack the Giant Killer, an old Cornish tale, was on my list and *The Plastic Dragon*. At the end of my stint I played a Cornish tune, and the room filled with piskies and fairies. Jack looked over at me and gave me the thumbs up, then shouted across the room. 'Don't worry about them. It happens all the time.' The rest of the revellers nodded reassuringly. I hesitated, unable to believe they could see what I saw.

'It's just the Piskies, Don. They like the music,' said Jack.

Once the room had cleared I asked about Toddy, but Landlord Jack had only been around the place for ten years.

'You'd need to ask Finley, he was here before me, and if anyone will remember, he will. Been around these parts all his life. Never hardly moved out of Polperro'

Finley lived in a fisherman's cottage close to the seashore and spent most of his time at his daughter Fiona's café, helping out. Jack took us there for lunch on Monday. Finley had the bright blue eyes of a thoroughbred Cornishman, clouding with age, however there was nothing cloudy about his memory.

'Toddy Oggy came to Cornwall the summer of '68. He was the greatest storyteller I'd ever seen. Magical! The piskies loved him; but he was a man who couldn't settle, always drifting off. Last I knew he'd gone to Land's End in search of Craggy Jackson. Looking for an old word, he said. What he meant by that I couldn't tell you, but Craggy Jackson was the oldest storyteller in Cornwall and someone suggested to Toddy that he might help. I expected him to come back, but never saw him again.'

It transpired that Craggy was still alive and lived in a trailer just a few miles away, having left Land's End some time ago. Jack and Fergus took us to see him. The trailer was more of a '60s Dormobile, painted yellow with flowers. Craggy was a sprightly man in his seventies with twinkling blue eyes. He was delighted to meet us and wanted to know all about Cotehill and Carlisle.

'Beautiful part of the world. Toddy often talked about Cotehill and Indigo in her cottage in the wood. He was very fond of his friends there and missed them a lot, but couldn't get back, poor man.'

Lisa and I exchanged glances, our quest just took a turn for the better.

'Why couldn't he get back, Mr. Craggy?' I asked, daring not to lose the moment.

'Call me Craggy, Don. It seemed he needed to find a word. He stayed with me for three weeks and we trawled through every story I knew, All the old ones, that is. Seems the word was one no longer used and hadn't been for at least three centuries. I have a few stories only I know, passed down from my great grand folk and never written. Stories like that often carry words from the original telling. He jotted down one or two.It was a great puzzle to me, but he said it was urgent to help the fairies in Cumbria. Well, that's no surprise to us storytellers, especially here in Cornwall where most of the population has seen a fairy. The upshot was that Toddy heard about a man in some remote part of Ireland whose words were pure old, and off he went to find him.'

'Could a sixteenth century story told in Ireland have any relevance to a spell cast in Cumbria, Don?' Lisa mused.

We were back home and planning the next trip.

Chapter 24

Ethna O'Flagherty

Before leaving for Ireland, I visited Mum and Dad. Dad didn't look well, and he told me he'd had the flu and was on the mend now.

'Donovan, it's good to see you. I wanted to talk to you about a few changes I've made in the factory.' I felt the glaze forming over my eyes. 'I know you have no interest in it, Son, not as it is now anyway, and I respect that. I've read the literature you handed out at the Blue Moon. It's a worrying state of affairs.'

Mum brought the quiche and chips and we moved to the dining table.

'Let me tell you my idea. I've had the boys in the lab look at the problem of plastic not being planet friendly, and believe me, I'm with you all the way with this Donovan, it's a curse. Your dragon story hit the nail on the head. With that in mind, I'm willing to invest whatever it takes to find a solution,to make plastic bio-degradable and planet friendly, and I know you're thinking it's too late and people like me should have been less greedy and more aware of the planet's needs, but it's never too late to make a start.'

I was listening hard.

'First, I will turn half of the factory into a recycling plant, the best in the world. You will be in charge. Secondly, my boys and the top in the field will work on changing the chemical make-up of plastic and seek a viable solution. Finally, fifty percent of profit will go towards cleaning up the mess we've made. I want you to oversee it all. Bring in whoever it takes. We start when you get back.'

Wow!

Back at the cottage, Lisa was packing for the journey to Ireland. It seemed the oldest storyteller in Ireland lived in Tipperary. so that's where we planned to start. But first, to Liverpool for the long boat trip.

~

'In ancient Celtic society, bards held a position of esteem, second only to kings. Bards memorized vast amounts of poetry which they performed live, and their poems and songs were often the only historical record available. Some may consider them to be historians. Bards evolved into storytellers called "seanchaí" who wandered from town to town. In this informal way, an ancient oral literary tradition continued into modern times.' Irish Central (online).

Simon had booked a few gigs across Ireland and I'd researched Irish stories to tell, as well as the Cumbrian and Cornish collection. It's from one of those stories we took your name, in fact.

We sailed on the midnight crossing and arrived early morning in Belfast. According to Lisa's research, a man called Padraig O'Leary was who we were looking for. If Toddy was looking for the oldest story teller, or teller of the oldest stories, this man could suggest who that may have been.

In Belfast I told the story of Lir whence came your name, Fionuala, about the jealous stepmother who turns the children into swans. I'd learned a few Irish jigs to play on the tin whistle, and told the plastic dragon tale. Sure enough Conan had somehow spread the news of my arrival and the fairies, the Tuatha de danaan and leprechauns, were out in force. I waited for Sean the landlord to tell me their presence was an everyday occurrence, but he didn't, so I assumed Lisa and I were the only people in the room who remembered seeing them.

From Belfast we went to Newcastle by the sea, overlooked by the Mountains of Mourn, then Bangor, Carrickfergus and finally Ballymena, where Padraig O'Leary awaited us. Lisa had written in advance about our quest and arranged to meet at the Lucky Clover Inn at midday on the final Saturday of our trip.

Padraig was a white-haired, jovial man in his sixties, his clothes were ragged, but that was his style and notably his shoes were bright red leather. Despite his odd attire, he had a sincere and thoughtful way about him.

'I never met Toddy, but heard of him from time to time on the storytelling circuit. Fine at his craft heard say. He left us a good collection from Cumbria and the Borderlands. Had some great Reiver Tales and King Arthur's Cumbrian and Cornish escapades. I've used some of them myself.' He told us he thought the storyteller Toddy would have seen was Ethna O'Flagherty. 'She was one of the greatest and had a stock of stories told her by her grandma, who got them from her grandma and so on. The stories she told were never written down, Ethna couldn't read or write, nor could the rest of her line. In 1962, she would have been ninety-eight, but her memory was still sharp. I remember listening to her stories many times and could recite any of them word for word.'

'Have you any idea where Toddy went when he left Ballymena?' I asked, hopeful for a lead.

'That's the thing, Don, he never left, but no-one knows where he is.'

To our despair, the plot just thickened.

'Toddy had been in Ballymena for a week, listening to Ethna's stories. Then one day he rushed into the post office with a big box, and said he needed to post it urgently. Neeve the postmistress sorted it out for him, and he rushed away. He was never seen in these parts again.'

'Which way did he rush? To the train station or into the hills? Did he have a car?' We needed a full investigation, and I believed the next step was to get the police involved. Northern Ireland was a volatile and dangerous place back then. I feared that maybe something very sinister had happened to Toddy.

'The police looked into it Don. Toddy was loved by the whole community. Those days storytellers brought some fantasy and escape from the troubles we faced. I suppose that's true of any era. That's why I became one.'

'Where did he send the package?' I asked although it was a long shot.

'He sent it to a village in Cumbria called Cotehill and addressed to Indigo Dune. I've been through the story many times with Neeve. She's always on about it.'

'Did she know what was in the package?'

'Yes, it was his top hat. The one he wore when storytelling, and his tin whistle.' A strange feeling crept over me. 'Neev had seen him a few times that week, telling stories at the Pot of Gold Club. She said it was a special hat and would light up different colours when he told his tales. The last time she saw him he had no hat or whistle, and when she asked him why not, he said he'd sent them home in case he lost them as they were precious.'

To say that I felt sick to the pit of my guts would be an understatement. The hat and whistle I used had been stored away inside a box in Granny's wardrobe, and when I moved into the cottage I found them and straight away and adopted them for my act. I was sure they were the same hat and whistle Toddy Oggy had posted from here all those years ago. But why?

Lisa's face was a picture of abject shock and horror; a fair reflection of my thoughts. The hat and whistle I'd so carelessly carted round the country as we searched for Toddy, belonged to Toddy, and for some reason he had hastily packed them off for Granny to look after.

That was to be our final night in Ireland and I had a gig at the Pot of Gold Club. Lisa and I discussed my wearing the hat and playing the tunes, and decided there was no way out as they were instrumental to the act.

'Especially the hat trick, Don. It's what got you where you are now,' Lisa said.

I shook my head, mystified.

The evening went well. Padraig was there and told one of Ethna's old stories for my benefit, and Lisa recorded it. My act was well received, and the plastic dragon drew thousands of eco warrior fairies to let me know the Northern Ireland branch was as active as the mainland in cleaning up the planet. Then, amongst the adulation and mirth, I saw a mirthless face. It was a sinister presence amidst good, and I recognised the incongruity of such malice amongst the joy. It was something bad, and I needed to react swiftly. But how?

I took Lisa by the hand and continued to smile and bow to the audience. As we bowed I whispered; 'we must leave now. I will trip the lights. Get your bag and stay close to me.'

Reaching behind the bandstand, I pulled the plugs and plunged the place into darkness, triggering gasps and groans from the audience, and we made for the door, ran to the car, jumped in and screeched away. I drove as fast as I could for the hills and didn't stop until we reached the ferry port. There we bought a ticket and by midnight were crossing the Irish Sea.

'Now will you tell me what happened?' Lisa asked, attempting to break my stony silence.

'I saw something bad,' was all I could say.

Chapter 25

Toddy's Hat

The farther we got from that place, the better I felt, and on Sunday evening we were back at Cotehill woods, baking potatoes and enjoying supper by the fireside.

It had been quite a journey, and we had returned with a lot to think about; the beauty of Ireland, Ethna's stories, Padraig, The Pot of Gold, the hat and whistle mystery, Toddy's strange behaviour just before he disappeared, and then the thing I didn't want to think about; the bad thing I decided to tuck away to where my thoughts would never go.

True to his word, Dad had made changes at work. I went in early Monday morning, excited to see how things were going. Dad showed me to my new office, which was pleasantly bright with plants of all sizes and hues, which made me feel I was in a garden rather than an office. Seems Dad understood me after all. Simon agreed to be co-manager of my unit. He'd proved himself a tireless organiser who could make things happen. He was also well known by the media as a spokesperson for the Kill the Plastic Dragon movement, which was gathering momentum across the country and not only in fairyland.

I got a few more friends from the old gang together. I'd known them most of my life and trusted their integrity. We met in my office once a week, and for the initial stages of our enterprise they travelled round the country and farther afield gathering recycling ideas from wherever they could. Meanwhile Dad fixed us up with a few Archimedes computers, and we were riding the techno wave.

Conan had appeared on the Sunday evening of our

return, to hear our Irish news. When I told him about Toddy's hat, he sat for a long time in thought.

'Why would he post it home? Was it because he'd given up on the storytelling? Or was it because someone was after it?' Conan mulled.

'Don, was there anything in the letters he sent to your granny? Any mention of the hat?' Lisa asked. And out came the letters. As we settled down to study them, Poppy arrived. I hadn't seen her for a long time and it was like a reunion with an old friend. So good to have her back in my house, she was such a positive force. The four of us studied the letters for any hint of a reference to Toddy's hat. We found no direct mention of it, but one or two hints in his letters from Ireland.

'I met with Ethna, she is the most amazing woman you could imagine (apart from yourself). At 91 years of age her memory is as clear as a bell, and the stories she tells of old Ireland are fascinating. Indigo, old friend, I think I may have found what I came here for, but there is something disturbing happening. I'll tell you about it when and if we meet again.'

His final letter from Ireland was short and to the point.

'I hope you receive the parcel? I can trust only you, It's in there, Indigo.' Your true and loving friend, Timothy.

We all assumed he was referring to the hat with the words; *It's in there*. But it told us nothing. We knew the hat was in the parcel, and I was still reeling from the news, since I'd been sporting it for quite a few years throughout my storytelling career.

'Where did he get the hat, I wonder?' said Lisa, shifting the speculation from what and why, to where was an interesting development.

'It belonged to an old magician friend of ours,' Conan said. 'He used to come to your granny's a lot. Michael Scott. He lived in the village, but sadly died. We were all devastated. He wanted Timothy to have his hat.'

'Michael Scott was a magician?' Lisa and I gasped in unison.

'So it's a magician's hat?' Lisa continued after the

significance of Michael Scott's name reoccurring in the folds of the mystery penetrated our consciousness. 'Don, fetch the hat.' I obeyed without question. Lisa was on to something. It was still in the car boot, so I rushed out into the late night. Strangely, the boot was open, but I thought nothing of it. I retrieved the hat and rushed back inside. Lisa took it from me.

'In his letter, Toddy wrote; *It's inside, Indigo*. What if he wasn't referring to the parcel, but to the hat?' As she spoke, she pushed and pulled at the inside of the hat and sure enough, the inner disc of the hat detached and out fell a torn piece of paper. There was a collective gasp.

I unfolded the paper and found a list of ten words I'd never encountered before.

'Don't speak them out loud,' Conan commanded. 'It's possible that one of these words is the one we need to save the tree. I must take them, Don. Not another soul must know about our find tonight.'

I wondered if I should mention the open boot, but decided not to, although my thoughts returned to the bad presence in the Ballymena Pot of Gold. Was there a connectionI wondered?

Lisa glanced at the words and I guessed she was memorising them. She had a photographic memory. Then she handed the paper to Conan. Poppy smiled her gentle smile.

'Well done both of you. If you've found the word that will save our tree, you'll be heroes forever after.' With that, they were gone.

~

The next few weeks were taken up with office work, storytelling and interviews with the newspapers and radio. Our trip through the UK had resulted in a lot of interest and support on a national scale, and Dad's new factory was offering a great deal of inspiration. New recycling ideas were created every day, and other cities copied Dad's idea, which was fine; we weren't in competition with anyone. The goal was to clean up the plastic and move forward in a more planet friendly way. We had visitors from the international community interested in our ideas, and Simon, my right-hand man, did a great job by introducing an educational wing, which welcomed schools to come along and trial the new recycling methods and bring their ideas.

We didn't see Conan for a while after he took the list of words, so felt that the search for Toddy was over. It was strange not to be on the case anymore, and we had no satisfactory ending, since we still didn't know what happened to him. We found the time to do some normal things like stroll around Bitts Park, as we called it, which was very close to my town house. We went to the cinema and the theatre. One day I proposed marriage to Lisa. I secretly set a table in the most beautiful part of Cotehill wood. It was April, and the bluebells carpeted the earth beneath the trees. I'd bought a sapphire ring the colour of the bluebells, and she accepted.

Each season the woods don their relevant garb and emerge resplendent, and I'd be hard pressed to choose a favourite, but the spring Lisa and I got engaged was the most amazing I can remember. The animals, birds and plants worked in harmony to create the most incredible landscape.

Life was busy. *The Plastic Dragon* was taking me into schools where the children were doing great things towards change. Simon still found time to manage the gigs and booked me in at the Glastonbury Festival that year.

One notable thing that happened was the recurrence of my horse dream. It was late spring, and I was at the cottage after a Saturday Blue Moon session. I went to bed and chatted to Lisa over the mobile for a while, then dropped off to sleep. The dream was the same; me riding a black horse at speed and the horse sweating and steaming from the nostrils. Riding and riding through a bleak landscape. When I awoke I was outside the cottage, lying on the grass with a pale blue dawn sky looking down at me. The cottage door was open, and I was wearing the pyjama trousers I had on when I went to bed. At least this time I didn't land in hospital. Still, I was unsure whether I'd just walked out of the cottage or had been somewhere.

Lisa agreed it was odd to have the same dream twice and find myself outside the cottage both times, especially when I had a clear memory of falling asleep in my bed.

She suggested I consult a dream therapist and looked one up for me. Her name was Oona Sands, and she had a little dream practice on Grey Street, just off London Road in

Carlisle. I made an appointment for the following day. To tell you the truth, the dream disturbed me I and worried about the fact I was waking up outside the cottage. I'd hardly slept for two nights.

Oona was a delicate, gentle woman, with skin as white as snow and soft brown doe-like eyes. She wore green silk which was the perfect colour to show off her thick mane of auburn hair. She invited me to relax in a huge comfy armchair and took position in its identical twin opposite.

'Now then Donovan, tell me about your dream, remembering every detail,' she urged, her voice like a slither of moonlight, softly lighting the way for the unsure and uncertain. I felt safe in her presence and delved deep into my unconscious to recall the dream.

'It's a hazy landscape, no colour, like a black and white film, all shades of grey and I'm on horseback galloping very fast. I can see my hands gripping the reins, they are gloved in leather. The horse is sweating, its black hair like shiny thick black oil. Its hooves are pounding the dry earth and dust flies up.'

'What do you see ahead of you in the dream, Don?' Oona asks gently.

'Only the horizon. It's flat and the grey earth meets the grey sky. There are no trees, it's like a dessert but no sun. No colour.' My voice sounds distant as I talk, but why would that be?

'Are you alone in the dream?' she asks.

I hesitate, because I'm not sure. The horse's hoofs are loud and there could be more than one set.

'Do you get the impression you're being chased in the dream?' asked Oona. I hadn't thought about it, but tried hard to remember how I felt, digging deeper and deeper until I remembered.

'Yes!' I cried. 'I am being chased, and there is a point in the dream, when the rider pulls up beside me. I glance to my left and he's there. I see his face, but don't know who it is.' And then I wake up outside the cottage.

'How does the face make you feel, Don?'

'It has no impact on me. I look at it and continue to gallop as fast as I can,' I say.

'Perhaps you're not being chased, in that case. Perhaps

he is riding with you. A companion. Don, there are a few interpretations of galloping horse dreams. Some say that if you are galloping on a black horse, misfortune will follow. Others say dreaming about galloping horses or a drove of horses running, suggest you are actively looking for a solution to a problem which will be solved, and you will see the dawn of life. It seems your dream has the effect of leading you to sleep walk. This is nothing to concern yourself about, and there are ways to overcome and control this behaviour. Do either of the scenarios I suggested fit your present state in life?'

'I suppose I can identify with the second one about solving a problem,' I answered, amused, but unable to explain why. I held back the story of Conan's lost word and the quest for Toddy Oggy. She may have me sectioned.

'I suggest you install cameras around your property to monitor your night time movements, they may tell you how often the sleep walking occurs. Drink something soothing before bed, a cup of coco perhaps. Would you like to make another appointment?'

I declined and paid the fee, not sure I agreed with her assessment, but the session had definitely clarified the dream for me. I felt no fear in the dream and the other rider was with me, not against me, which was reassuring. What it all meant I couldn't say, and I suspected there would be a recurrence, but for now I felt better and more ready to fall asleep, especially after a cup of the recommended coco.

Chapter 26

Glastonbury

The wedding plans were underway. Lisa and I wanted a simple, rural affair. A Midsummer night's wedding in the woods, with a bonfire and fireworks to celebrate. Lisa's parents were more for a ceremony at Carlisle Cathedral. Her Dad was high up in the city officialdom and wanted the 'best' for his daughter. Lisa wanted a floaty, ivory silk affair for the dress, her Mum wanted a huge, magnificent creation with a thirty-foot long train and ten bridesmaids. My dad wanted a fleet of vintage Rolls Royce, and we wanted horses and carriages.

The wedding plans were a disaster.

Lisa and her mum poured over copies of *Bride* magazine, and every week the plans changed. Lisa's Mum was a strong-minded person and Lisa was an only child, so our wedding was receiving her full attention. The venue was finally decided as Saint John's church in the village. A pretty old church which overlooks the hills and farmland we both were fond of. The reception would be held at The Greyhound Inn and the Village Hall, then back to the cottage for a the bonfire and fireworks. We were all happy with the plans and began to look forward to the day, which fell two days after the Glastonbury gig, as that was the only available date we could book the church.

Lisa decided she'd rather not go to Glastonbury and would stay around for final preparations.

It seemed *The Plastic Dragon* was now being sold at almost every school around the country, and a book company contacted me offering a contract and illustrator. This was exciting news and a great way to get the message out there.

Things on the Conan front had been unusually quiet. He hadn't visited for a while and I was secretly worried. I at the least expected an update re: the fairyland tree, but I guessed all was well and he had no need for us anymore, which in a way was a good thing, but I missed him.

Meanwhile, the work on the book began with a few examples of illustrations for me to peruse. Lisa and I decided on a traditional style with a contemporary twist, and were super excited.

It was an altogether exciting time. The week of the wedding and Glasto soon arrived, and I left Lisa arranging flowers and strings of fairy lights around the cottage.

~

Simon couldn't make it to Glastonbury as he was in Amsterdam on an eco-mission. The drive down from Cumbria late on Thursday was uneventful, but there was a rain-laden sky and I hoped the tent Simon had fixed me up with was waterproof. Back then Glastonbury punters weren't as pampered as today. The big corporations hadn't cottoned on to the potential for advertising and profit. The festival hadbecome a platform for the anti-nuclear campaigners CND, and there were lots of banners and badges. I pitched the tent just before the rain started. Luckily Lisa had packed a pile of sandwiches and some drinks, because when the rain started it was impossible to go anywhere. I stayed in the tent for a long time as the relentless rain pounded. It turned out to be the wettest day for forty-five years. When it eventually stopped, I went out to join the muddy throng. They scheduled Van Morrison to play together with The Chieftains, Sad Café and Jackson Browne, so I expected some good times between story telling.

I let the organisers know who I was, and they showed me where I could pitch my story telling tent. It was close to the theatre tent and a few alternative services on offer, like astrology and reflexology, where *Cosmic Feet* were the thing. I thought that was the name of a band. but turns out the *cosmic feet* were what they would provide for you, were you to visit their tent.

Simon had kindly produced posters and leaflets for me to advertise:

Cumbrian Story-Teller and Author of The Plastic Dragon
Donovan Draper
Stories and tin whistle melodies
3:00 pm-4:00pm
7:00pm-8:00pm
11:00PM-Midnight
Take a Flight of Fantasy.

I liked that he had left me some time to enjoy the festival, so put the sign up and went for a wander. The sun was out on Saturday and the atmosphere, good. Thousands of folk out to enjoy music can't ever be a bad thing.

Glastonbury Tor is popular with the fairy folk, and has lots of interesting story generators with its connections to early Christianity, Arthurian legends, the Isle of Avalon, and the doorway to Annwn - the Celtic otherworld. One of its most famous fairy stories is that of the meeting between St Collen and Gwyn ap Nudd, King of the fairy folk and Lord of Annwn. I wondered if the fairies would know I was around. It had been so long since any contact with Conan, I started to think it had all been a dream and the quest for Toddy Ogden a figment of my imagination.

I bought myself a CND t-shirt and returned to my tent, which was a six-person, tall enough for me to stand up. I had a few camper chairs for the comfort of my audience; only expecting a handful. However, just before the four o'clock gig, the organisers informed me I was a sell out and many people with young children would come to hear *The Plastic Dragon*. It went well and to my surprise the Glastonbury fairies came along to cheer me on.

The eight p.m. gig was just as busy, but fewer children came. The camping chairs I'd brought were pathetically inadequate, but the punters were happy to sit on the grass outside the tent. I had prepared the story of Saint Collen and Gwin app Nudd, King, of the fairies, with some particularly nifty tin whistle tunes of Celtic origin.

It was nine-thirty p.m. before I could get away that night, as I had an encore and told another old Cumbrian tale of King Arthur. It felt magical to tell my stories in the same field Van Morrison was playing, and the peace activists were out in force; Glastonbury must be one of the best gigs possible.

There was a storyteller two tents away from mine, who drew a huge crowd. I hoped to catch his act, but was too late.

Maybe later.

Everyone was happy at Glasto, not a grumpy face in sight, and I feasted on the ambiance, wandering from act to act and browsing the stalls.

Eleven o'clock came round and a smaller audience gathered to hear my tales. These were the hardcore of the storytelling world. The ones who never missed a chance to hear a good yarn. My stories were well received and a few folks hung around afterwards to talk.

'Nice act, Don, quite magical. Anyone who can bring out the fairies like that, is worth his salt and the hat thing is terrific,' said a large woman wearing a bright orange head dress. Her friends nodded agreement. 'We're the Glastonbury Storytellers' Guild,' she added.

'Thanks ladies, pleased to meet you. Interesting to know you have a Guild,' I responded. But I was too sleepy for a long talk, so set about packing my stuff.

'Get in touch if you're in these parts again, I'm Gloria and this is Roxy and Scarlet,' she said, shaking my hand.

'Will do!' I called as they walked away. I carried the camper chairs into the tent and heard them commenting as they went; 'He's almost as good as Toddy,' Gloria remarked. Dropping the chairs, I rushed out of the tent and into the music filled night, calling her name; 'Gloria! Gloria!' But there was no sign of Gloria or her friends.

When I returned to my tent, I found that Lisa had called my mobile several times. I phoned her, but it was one in the morning by then and she was sleeping.

Chapter 27

Toddy Oggy and Grey Land

My sleep was fitful, as I had Gloria's comment on my mind and tried to imagine ways she could know Toddy. As a member of the Storyteller's Guild, she would come across many of our number. She was too young to have seen Toddy live, as he hadn't performed since the sixties, or so we thought.

What was going on?

Just as I'd fallen asleep, my phone rang, and it was Lisa. 'D n C n n c m l t w d d g r' she said.

'What?' I shouted.

'C n lt wd has gn' She went on.

'I can't hear you, the reception's bad' I shouted.

Lisa hung up.

After a breakfast of muesli and milk, I went for a stroll around the site, half expecting to see Gloria or Scarlet or Roxy, but no luck, so I planned to visit the Storytellers' Guild before heading back to Cotehill. Meanwhile, I'd freshen up and lean in on another day at Glastonbury.

After the eleven o'clock gig, I was signing autographs, feeling famous, when a tall, thin middle-aged man passed me his programme to sign. I smiled and signed.

'Where did you get that hat?' he asked.

'Long story mate,' I answered. 'It belonged to a magician called Michael Scott, then to a storyteller called Toddy Oggy, then to my granny called Indigo, and now it's mine.'

The man put his hand out. Good to meet you, Donovan. I'm Toddy Oggy, or Timothy Ogden if you want the formal version.' We shook hands and yes, I was speechless.

After the abject shock of seeing the man in the flesh, I insisted that he tell me every detail of the story, but it was a long one, so we sat under the stars on the hill, while the late band played and he revealed all.

'Well, Don, I was on the mission for Conan, my good friend, and I'd been all over trying to find his infernal old word, pardon my saying, but I was fond of the chap and wanted to help the tree in fairyland and save the Cotehill branch. So I was at Allonby, Keswick, Cornwall and finally took myself off to Ireland to meet Ethna, whose stories are a thousand years old. I listened to all her stories and wrote ten words that have been totally lost to the English language. We storytellers know this things, as words are what we deal in, they're our currency, so I know an obsolete word when I hear one. Anyway, I wrote them down and hid the list in a secret compartment in that hat of mine... or yours if you prefer. Michael Scott gave me the hat before he died. He'd been searching for the word when he got sick; but that's another story.' I blinked, possibly for the first time since he started to tell the tale. Michael Scott was in on it! 'Now, Conan had warned me that the bad ones could try to get the words from me, and two things happened. Firstly, I fell in love with a girl from Dublin and second, I felt an evil presence in my lodgings, so I sent the hat to Indigo immediately, and then ran off with Mary to Dublin. Mary and I married soon after and are still together after over thirty years. I couldn't be open about the words inside the hat because of the bad ones. Are they still there or did Indigo find them?' he asked. Looking at the hat which lay beside me.

The answer wasn't that simple, as you know. I related my side of the story, to his dismay. He was astounded to hear that the words took so long in reaching Conan and impressed by Lisa's genius in eventually finding them.

We parted company as the dawn broke, arranging to meet again at my tent for breakfast at ten in the morning, Glastonbury was over, and we had to vacate the field by midday Monday.

Back at my tent Lisa had again been trying to contact me. This time there was a text message, it read; 'Conan lost the words. They disappeared. I only remember five, but all useless.'

WHAT!!!

Had it all been for nothing? I asked myself as a bright red sun rose behind the hillside. We can't start again. Then a thought emerged from the fog of my tired brain. Toddy was here. He may remember the words. It was our last hope. Meanwhile, I needed to sleep; I had a long drive home later that day, and in three days timeI was getting married.

Before my head hit the pillow, I sent a text to Lisa. It read; 'Toddy is here. All is revealed. Will see him later to ask about words. Very careless of Conan, Love you! Good night.'

Send.

My head hit the pillow.

On waking, my first thought was that I'd slept through the whole day and it was night time again, because it was dark, so I panicked; I'd missed Toddy and should be on my way home to Lisa and the wedding. Scrambling out of the tent, it seemed someone had moved my tent to a different place. I expected to see the field and hillside, but there was a wall. The cheek of it, I thought. The organisers must have ejected me from the site while I slept and plonked me beside this wall. How dare they? And where's my car?

Now on my feet I looked more closely at my surroundings and decided I was dreaming again. Everything was grey or black or pale grey. It was the colourless landscape of my dream, except this time I wasn't on horseback. I waited to wake up, then pinched myself, but was still there. As far as the eye could see the wall continued and inside the wall, apart from me, was very little to speak of; grey grass, a flat landscape and grey sky. This was like no place I had ever seen before, and it was worrying.

'Donovan, no need to be afraid,' a small voice said. 'I swung round and there was a little man, not unlike Conan. 'It's good of you to visit again and we hope you'll stay' he continued.

'Sorry, I can't stay. Which is the way back please?' I ventured, attempting to hide my fear.

'The way back? You might try climbing the wall, or walking for miles and miles that way, or that way,' he pointed in two equally flat and endless directions. 'Or you could come with me and forget about ever getting out. That's the easy way.'

I followed him. Soon a grey castle appeared in the flat distance and as we approached it, the little man talked. 'My name is Bronan, I'm sure you need an explanation as to why you're here. It won't be forever, Don, fifty years tops,' he said cheerfully. My heart sank and sank and sank until it could sink no more. Fifty years!

'Look Bronan! I'm getting married in three days. Let me out of here!' I hissed.

'Sorry about the wedding, but you have to stay about fifty years. You'll get used to it and Lisa will get over it, she's a resourceful lady.'

WHAT?

He knew Lisa?

The castle was just ahead of us, looming. 'I'm Conan's brother, Don, I know everything about you and Lisa. The truth is, Conan and I had a huge bust up about four centuries ago, your time, much less in fairy time. It was all over one of King Arthur's Knights who wanted to marry a friend of ours, who happens to be a witch. Conan was against the marriage and turned the Knight against her, so she put a curse on him. I was all for the marriage. They seemed like a compatible couple, but being his brother I was caught up in the curse, So I begged the witch and she freed me from Conan's curse, but said the Cotehill branch of fairies would expire, with their tree, unless Conan's curse could be reversed. She also said that if it is reversed, then I would be cursed. So, Don, the reason you're here is because Toddy is the only person who knows the word that can reverse the curse, and you were about to pass that information on to him so we had to remove you from the equation. Just until the tree dies and the Cotehill fairies are extinct.'

I was horrified. This was Conan's brother?

'How can you behave that way towards your brother?' I asked, angry now to think anyone would so callously want to exterminate the Cotehill fairies.

'Conan is cursed to everlastingly helping people. I could never live like that and refuse to be exposed to it. Once the tree dies, I'll be safe.'

This was too much. How selfish!

'Listen, Don. Life's not too bad here. Once you get used to the lack of colour. Who needs colour anyway? It's overrated. You may shake your head, but you'll soon learn.'

Hopefully, I'd wake up soon. This had to be a dream of the worst kind. I followed Bronan across the drawbridge and into the castle. Immediately the bridge was pulled up, and I was trapped. 'This will be your room during your stay and Sol here will look after you.' I looked at Sol whose eyes were the saddest eyes I've ever witnessed. He was draped in a grey, sack-like tunic and stood barefoot and silent. 'We want you to be comfortable. None of this is your fault, I know, and you're free to walk around the grounds as much as you like.'

My room was cell like with barred, high windows and a grey stone bed. I longed for some colour and freedom, and Lisa. I lay on the grey stone bed and stared at the grey stone ceiling feeling there was no way out. There could be no way out. Nobody knew I was here and nobody knew where this place was. It was negativity land, the exact opposite to fairyland, and why would anyone be here just to avoid having to help people? I closed my eyes and tried to imagine Lisa and what she would be doing now. Arranging flowers in the church, gathering sticks for the bonfire, just being her lovely positive self. Sad Sol brought me a tray of grey food.

'How long have you been here?' I asked Sol, but he didn't respond; he placed the tray on the grey, stone table beside the bed and shuffled out. His sadness was infectious and, leaving the grey, gloopy excuse for food, I lay on the hard bed and plunged into the depths of sadness.

There was a sound like thunder and the castle rocked. Earthquake! I thought. Then two giant, black horses broke through the wall and a hand grabbed me and swung me onto the back of one of them. I clung on. I knew this part. The horses galloped and galloped through the castle walls and the grey landscape. Sweating and steaming from the nostrils the horse behind me galloped and caught up, I glance to my left and saw its rider. It was Toddy. The horses galloped and galloped through the castle wall and on across the grey landscape towards the grey horizon.

'We mustn't stop!' shouted Toddy. Keep going. It seemed like forever and then far into the distance a tiny dot of colour appeared and as we galloped, it grew and grew. We galloped on and the horses carried us towards the colour until finally we reached the edge of the grey and with a huge leap we crossed it and were back to green hills, bright sunshine and blue sky. We galloped on.

'Can't stop yet!' Toddy shouted, and on we went, until we reached a forest where the horses slowed to a trot and finally stopped to let us down.

Sometimes I wonder what would have happened had Toddy not saved me; how my life may have passed me by in that grey world with Sol and Bronan always there to remind me of Conan, my cottage, Lisa, and how it would have been for Lisa; waiting for my return like a Cumbrian Miss Faversham in her wedding dress. It makes me shudder to think of how it might have been.

Toddy and I walked silently over the brow of the hill where I was amazed and relieved to see Glastonbury stretched before me. The stage was dismantled, litter pickers busy clearing up, and my car parked beside the tent. All was normal.

We found a coffee stall serving sleepy stragglers and settled for a rickety table.

'OK, Toddy. Please begin. Tell me what just happened, how you knew my whereabouts and where the horses came from. I think you have a lot of explaining.' He faced me at the table, long fingers wrapped around the cup of hot coffee, long legs outstretched and crossed at the ankles. His long white hair was tied at the back and he wore a green bandana.

'Don, it's so complicated, even I'm confused, but I'll try to make it as clear as possible.'

And so, as Glastonbury was tidied away for another year, I listened to Toddy repeat a lot of stuff I already knew about the lost word, Cornwall, Ballymena, Michael's hat, posting the hat to Indigo, until he reached the parts I didn't know.

'Back in the sixties Michael and your dad tried to help Conan and also found themselves trapped by Bronan in the grey world. Conan sent me in to get them. He provided the horses and they carried me off. They knew where to go. I saved them, but Michael fell ill and died soon after, and your dad blamed Conan. When you didn't turn up yesterday I went looking for you. Your Motorola phone was on the pillow in your tent, and I read Lisa's messages. I knew they'd want you out of the way so you couldn't get the words from me, so I contacted Conan in the old way we used to, which is top secret, and he sent the horses. The rest is history.'

'It may be history, Toddy, but don't forget they'll still be after us. We need to leave here sharpish! Can you use your secret contact method again and let Conan know we're on our way? Maybe he'll send the horses?' I said.

'No, they only know the way to the grey world and back,' sighed Toddy. 'I could post the words to your cottage again. That would put Lisa in danger.'

Finally, Toddy messaged Conan, and we set off in my car. My phone battery had now died and I needed to find a place to recharge so I could phone Lisa, who must be frantic. The wedding was in two days' time and she had expected me home two hours ago. I was still dazed by events, but adrenalin was high, so I willed myself to keep going. At the first service station we came to, we stopped for another coffee and to charge my phone at a socket behind the counter. Mobile technology was still in its infancy so we had no phone ports or such like. While it was charging, I phoned Lisa from a phone box, but there was no reply.

After half an hour we set off again heading for the M6. As we drove, Toddy talked about my granny; 'I knew Indigo when we were at school together. She was a wonderful person, with a great creative streak. As children we'd spend a lot of time in the woods and your great granny Ruby would treat us to a spread of goodies before we went home. Seth, your great, great granddad, was around in those days and he was quite a character. It was Seth that introduced us to Conan and the other fairies. We knew them so well it didn't seem strange. After Michael's death your dad wanted no more to do with them, so when you came along Indigo was very discrete. However, we were all caught up in the quest in one way or another, and cared deeply about the Cotehill fairies and their tree.'

As I drove and listened to the complicated history of my cottage, I noticed a few posters advertising Plastic Dragon events, and thought about the book that would soon be published. It seemed strange that only a few days ago life was so much simpler and we were looking forward to the wedding and the book illustrations coming through, but now, here I was, an escapee from the grey world, speeding up the motorway with some obsolete words to save the Cotehill branch of Fairyland. I sighed at the thought of it all.

Then a strange thing happened. Each side of our motorway lane became lined by hosts of fairies; they met in the middle to form a tunnel. Fairies and elves of every kind. They created safe passage for us as we drove through Lancashire and through the Cumbrian hills.

'This'll be Conan's doing,' said Toddy. 'He's sent the message along the fairy grapevine to make sure we get home safely.'

The sight was one I'll never forget as long as I live, and it reminded me how special the fairy folk are and how much I cared that they would not be harmed by a spell cast ions ago by a love lorn witch. King Arthur's Knights had a lot to answer for, and Conan and the Cotehill fairies had been caught up in their petty dispute. I looked at Toddy, who had spent so many years in exile. Hiding in Ireland because of the situation. He was an old man now, and when he left thirty years ago, he left behind people who cared for him. Meg and Indigo, for a start, and Conan and the fairies. All those storytelling years lost. I realized, as we drove through the fairy tunnel, how special this was for him. His homecoming. He looked emotional, as if he was thinking the same things. Meanwhile, it seemed as if every fairy from every branch of fairyland along our route was out in force.

At last we arrived at the cottage and our tunnel vanished. I'd only been away four days, and it seemed like an eternity. I never would have thought I'd be arriving home with Toddy in tow and a brief spell in grey land to ponder on, let alone having met Bronan and sad Sol.

The cottage was a mass of floral glory. June is the most amazing month for forest life. The trees and flowers are bloomed in abundance and Lisa had festooned the cottage with flowers and fairy lights. There was a long table in the garden ready for the after party. However, there was no sign of Lisa. Inside the cottage was equally glorious with displays of fresh flowers everywhere. Toddy had to bend double to fit inside, and I could see his eyes fill with tears.

'It's been so long, Don.'

It was around five in the afternoon on Tuesday and I was pondering Lisa's whereabouts. She still wasn't answering her phone. There was ham and cheese in the fridge, so I fixed us some food and we ate at the table in the garden. Now the thing foremost in my mind at this point was my wedding, which was to be the next day. I called the library to ask if Lisa was there but they told me she hadn't been in for two days as she was taking a break to prepare for the big day. I wondered if I should be worried, so phoned her mum, who seemed to think she was in town with friends, enjoying her final day of freedom. Then Conan appeared. He looked dishevelled, but greeted us warmly.

'Toddy! It's the most glorious of days, now that you are back in Cotehill where we've all missed you beyond measure. Don! Our hero, how was Glasto? Don't answer that. I know all about it. You met my brother Bronan I believe, and visited Grey Land. I'll wipe the memory from you soon, but for now you need to remember. Follow me please, my two dearest human beings, and don't worry about Lisa, she'll be fine as long as everything goes according to plan.' This last comment startled me and I was just about to question it when we reached the strange part of the wood, the part I couldn't recall ever seeing before.

'We're in fairyland now.' Toddy informed me. 'We crossed into another dimension at the last oak tree. I remember it well.'

Conan smiled and looked around him. 'Those were the days, Toddy, when Indigo and Ruby and Seth were around and you children would spend the day in the woods playing games with us fairy folk. We often talk about the wonderful storyteller you became and the magical nights around the bonfire.'

'I seem to recall you were the one that brought the magic along, Conan.' They laughed together over this. Although the fairy wood was even more astounding than the real wood, I was too worried to enjoy it. I needed to see Lisa.

In time, we reached the ancient fairy oak, the root of all the problems. A host of fairies surrounded the tree, which glowed every colour of the rainbow. Two wizards joined us and invited us to sit upon the grass. There was an air of solemnity around the place.

'Toddy, we believe you have several most obsolete

words in the English language and as you know, we need them to break the spell which will destroy the Cotehill branch. The bad ones corrupted the words Lisa found in the hat in some way; when I returned with them to the tree, four of your words were missing, Toddy. We have the spell here, so we can try them immediately.' Toddy studied the list of words the wizards had and nodded emphatically. The wizards produced a scroll and unrolled it. One stood up like an orator and asked Toddy to insert a word on cue.

'*Snakes and lizards. Toadies gizzards. The tree will die.In a hundred...*' he points to Toddy; '*Slubberdegulion*' Toddy said.

Nothing happened.

'Again' said the wizard.

'*Snakes and lizards. Toadies gizzards. The tree will die in...*' he points to Toddy; '*Mawk*' offered Toddy.

Nothing.

'Again' said the wizard.

'*Snakes and lizards. Toadies gizzards. The tree will die in...*' A huge bat swept down on us and covered Toddy's face, clinging to it, so that Toddy couldn't speak. There was a collective gasp and Toddy writhed, his long legs stumbling blindly as he tore at the bat frantically, but couldn't remove it. I pulled out my torch and shone it in the bat's eyes and it loosened its grip.

'*Zenzizenzizenzic!*' Toddy called out. Collectively we looked puzzled.

'Please repeat,' said the wizard, leaning in to Toddy's bat covered face. He didn't need to repeat it. In the distance there came a rumbling which grew louder and louder and louder. Rumbling and rumbling until it became a deafening and terrifying roar, and a plume of black smoke appeared from the tree. It horrified us, thinking the tree was burning, but the plume ascended into the atmosphere and floated off to space, as far as we knew.

'The spell has lifted!' The wizard cried, after a brief examination of the tree. 'That was an amazing word, Toddy!'

'Yes,' said Toddy proudly.

You can imagine the ball that ensued. Every Cotehill fairy arrived, overjoyed that the tree was safe, and we were heroes.

'Conan, I really must get back,' I whispered, not wanting to be a killjoy.

'Absolutely, Don boy!' We made our way towards the last oak tree, and re-entered the real world... or the world as we know it, I should say.

'I'll leave you here if that's all right,' said Conan. 'Thanks for everything and don't worry about a thing; Lisa's fine, you'll probably never see Bronan again, and your quest for Timothy is over, but you haven't seen the last of me. There's still one little favour I'd like to ask of you, but not now. It can wait.'

At this my heart sank, just a little, but I refused to dwell on his words. I was desperate to see Lisa.

Toddy and I walked through the woods as if we'd been friends for years. He knew the woods as well as I did, and could name every tree and flower. Fairy lights greeted us as dusk fell at the cottage. There was a perfume of night-scented stock and honeysuckle wafting in the light breeze, and Lisa stood at the door awaiting my arrival, lovely in a long blue floaty dress. We hugged like we'd been apart forever, and she was overjoyed to meet Toddy, whom we invited to the wedding. We also invited him to stay overnight at the cottage, but he insisted on leaving to find a hotel in Carlisle as he was feeling weary and needed to smarten up. He borrowed Ivanhoe, which made me a little nervous, given his reputation for disappearing, but it seemed the decent thing to do.

Lisa and I talked well into the night, and I gave her a lift home. Our next meeting would be at the wedding and I hadn't fully shaken off the shock of my encounter with the Grey Land. I needed time to absorb the aroma of the woods and the ambience of my cottage.

There were many messages on my mobile when I charged it up again. Mum and Simon had been trying to contact me, and an unknown number; probably some cold caller.

I showered and went to bed.

Chapter 28

Woodland Magic

A glorious sun woke me at dawn after a sound sleep; no horses or grey lands, to my relief. Conan had forgotten to erase the memory of those things.

Lisa had stocked the cupboards and fridge with enough food to keep a small army alive for a year. I breakfasted at the garden table, enchanted by the colours and birdsong. The wedding was at eleven o'clock, so there was time for a stroll along the woodland path to where the fairy line was visible at night. It seemed so long since I'd thought about the plastic dragon and my job at Dad's new improved factory. A strange sensation visited me at that point. I felt responsible. I felt I had a mission to fulfil, and I would soon be Lisa's husband.

I thought about my Mum, Granny Indigo and her Mum and Dad, Ruby and Seth, who built the cottage, and the time they spent in the wood. Granny had taught me everything I knew about the place, the names of trees, plants, butterflies and insects. She showed me the worms and snails and slugs and the birds' nests with their tiny, fragile eggs. Hansel and Gretel lived there, she told me all the stories I knew then, until the woods filled not only with the birds, plants and animals I knew, but they were also populated by the characters from her stories; Little Red Riding Hood, the wolf, the woodcutter, the three bears, Goldilocks, King Arthur and his Knights, the various witches that popped up from time to time and all their deeds and wishes and misdemeanours were there in the wood, beanstalks and giants, princesses and frogs that turned to princes. I learned many of life's lessons listening to her stories, she would always emphasise the wisdom at the end. No matter what horrors went before, they lived happily ever after; they married the girl/man of their dreams; they slayed the dragon/giant/bad witch. We created such magical memories in that simple, humble place when Granny Indigo was alive.

Chapter 29

A Fairy Tale Wedding

The wedding went like a midsummer's day dream. Simon, my Best Man made us all laugh. Toddy, to my relief, arrived on Ivanhoe and told a story of how he'd met a brownie in Cotehill wood, who sent him on a mission to find an obsolete word, which most of the audience appreciated, but Lisa and I felt was a little near the knuckle. Lisa looked like a fairy tale princess in a silk, ivory dress and headdress decorated with wild flowers from the garden. I wore a dapper white suit and green waistcoat, also decorated with wild flowers from the garden. Mum and Dad smiled benignly throughout, and Lisa's folks seemed happy with their daughter's no frills wedding day. We wined and dined till late, then sang and danced around the fire and were in awe of the sparklers Mum brought along.

At the height of the celebrations the Cotehill branch emerged from the woods, singing a song that mesmerised us all and waved wands as bright as any sparkler. They stayed a while amongst our guests until, in an instant, they were gone, together with the memory of their presence for all but three at the gathering. It surprised me Conan didn't show up, but I guessed he had other fish to fry. It was kind of the fairies to join our celebration.

Lisa and I spent our honeymoon travelling around Cumbria. We drove to Wastewater, the most beautiful and haunting of the Lakes overlooked by Scafell Pike, the highest mountain in England. We travelled back along the Pass, and watched sunrises and misty mountains, swans on Lake Windermere and the houses of Beatrix Potter and William

Wordsworth. We climbed Mounts Skiddaw and Blencathra, andcreated our own story around wonderful Cumbria until it was time to return to the humdrum life of Cotehill wood. At least I was hoping for humdrum, but couldn't quite forget Conan's final words before we parted; 'There's just one more favour I need of you...' Those words didn't smack of finality, and it worried me, but I didn't tell Lisa.

However, there was humdrum for a while, when Lisa and I returned to work and the book publishing process continued its course. *The Plastic Dragon* was becoming popular worldwide, and I got invitations from far afield to discuss the plastic problem and the solutions we were trialling at Dad's factory. The Blue Moon gig every Wednesday was always a highlight of the week, with the regular band and other acts that came and went. It was more than just a gig, for me it was a source of inspiration being amongst the people I admired. After a few weeks, Toddy and his wife Mary moved back to Cotehill, to live in a house Toddy bought on the edge of the village. He landed a regular spot at the Blue Moon, and we'd often get together and plan our acts. We sometimes did a double act, which the punters really liked.

A year passed in this way and I seldom thought about Conan and Poppy, or Bronan and Grey Land. It was all dreamlike, although I knew it wasn't a dream.

Also Fionuala, you began your journey to join us. Lisa was to become your mum.

Chapter 30

A Package for Franz

They published *The Plastic Dragon* in the spring of '93, and it flew off the shelves. It went to China, Japan, India, America, Vietnam, Armenia; everyone wanted a copy and everyone wanted to kill the plastic dragon. By then there were more awareness campaigns to curb air and water pollution, to save the rain forests and to prevent acid rain, and the good people of the planet strove harder and harder to save it. The fairies continued to work in the woods. I often saw their glowing line relentlessly clearing up and it inspired me to carry on.

Dad's factory became a beacon of progress in the fight and attracted visiting scientists from all over the world. I enjoyed being there. It felt like the cutting edge of everything we needed to do to keep our planet safe from the relentless scourge of greed in the guise of progress.

Simon planned a book tour which would involve me and a few scientists travelling to Europe to spread the word. I wasn't keen to leave Lisa, but she had her work to do and was happy to stay behind. The first stop would be Germany.

'Home of the brothers Grimm,' I said as Simon passed me the ferry tickets. 'The perfect place for a storyteller.'

'Only if you speak German,' Simon laughed.

'I'll manage somehow,' I said, not very convinced. However, the book was out in Germany and the message had taken off there. Simon had booked several storytelling gigs along The Fairy Tale road, which traces the journey of brothers Jacob and Wilhelm Grimm, and Toddy was coming along. He got hold of an old camper van and painted it with fairy tale characters, and even gave us a name; *The Cumbrian Bards*.

The scientists Liam and Rory, chosen not only for their scientific knowledge, important for the plastic meetings we'd be attending, but also for their appreciation of stories. It would be impossible to travel in a camper van for three weeks on a storytelling trail with people who had no inkling of the importance of stories. Simon had also arranged for us to meet one of the oldest story tellers along the trail.

Simon read to us at length from the brochure he had procured from the local travel agency. He'd collected many maps to take along the route, and Lisa raided the library shelves for information about the brothers and their mission to gather tales from the people (volk) of Germany.

'In 1791, the family of the district magistrate, Grimm, moved to Steinau and into the magistrate's house which was over 200 years old. That's where you'll head to first; I've booked you in for two sessions at the library there and one at a folk club. They're having a plastic rally to coincide with your visit.'

It was the evening before we set off, early July and I was packing a few things into the van and making sure I had all the notes needed for the tour, when Conan appeared.

'Germany, Don, very nice!' I was surprised but happy to see him again. He looked less dishevelled than usual, his beard was neater and hair seemed less tangled.

'Conan! Good to see you, pal' I said, genuinely pleased. 'You look well.'

'I've a few distant cousins over there, I wonder if you'd mind doing me that favour?'

He didn't seem interested in niceties. 'When you arrive at Steinau, an elf called Franz will meet you. Please give him this package. It is a gift from the Cotehill branch. He'll take care of you over there.' He handed me the package and was gone.

I felt miffed. I hadn't seen him for over a year and he missed our wedding, but thinks it's fine to pop up out of nowhere with a package for an elf called Franz in Steinau, as if I didn't have enough to think about with a kill the plastic and tell stories tour ahead of me. I stashed the package in the glove compartment.

Toddy and the scientists arrived early the next day, and we tied our luggage to the roof of the newly named Gretel, the camper van. Gretel looked splendid, Toddy had done a great job with the paintwork and as we drove through Cumbria, we had lots of thumbs up from the folk there. A boat took us to the Hook of Holland, and from there we headed for Germany.

We took turns with the drive, studying Simon's maps and reading books about the Grimms, as well as delving into their stories. Liam and Rory seemed to enjoy doffing their scientist's hats for a while, and entered the spirit of fantasy. Lisa had done us proud with the selection of books she'd packed for us to devour along the way, together with ample sandwiches and mum's quiche.

We arrived late to Steinau and had no trouble finding the hotel. Steinau is a real fairy tale town; tall black and white houses, pretty roofs and higgledy piggledy roads. Our hotel overlooked the square, and I remember thinking how pretty Gretal looked parked outside. Check-in was efficient and before long my head hit the pillow and, with that wonderful feeling you get when the long journey is behind you and there are only good times ahead, I fell asleep.

Music woke me and it was daylight. My phone was ringing; Lisa required an update. I had nothing to say yet, but one look out of the window told me I'd have plenty to say later.

'Thanks for the books,' I mustered. 'We're all experts on the Bro's Grimm now. How's life at Cotehill?'

'Much as you left it yesterday,' said Lisa. We continued our non-conversation for as long as seemed decent and hung up with the promise I'd phone later with more interesting news.

Toddy and the scientists were already at breakfast when I arrived and we enjoyed hearty plates of ham and cheese. The first stop that day was the library.

Gretel patiently awaited our arrival, looking bright and jolly. We piled in with our gear, and Toddy drove the short distance to our destination where a small gathering waited. There were children and adults toting *The Plastic Dragon* and waiting for autographs. I obliged, and Toddy and I told our stories in the old library. Toddy wore his striped purple and green trousers and matching jacket, with a yellow shirt and red top hat. I was much less flamboyant in my jeans and a Plastic Dragon t-shirt emblazoned with the words; *Be Fantastic*

Recycle the Plastic, and Toddy's old hat - once Michael's old hat. It had too much history to leave behind.

We told stories from Cumbria, Northumberland and Yorkshire to the townsfolk, with the help of Wilhelm the translator who did a great job, and the people enjoyed our repertoire. Finally, with special lighting effects, I told the Plastic Dragon tale, which received a standing ovation and a huge collection of waste plastic was placed beside me for a photo. Unbelievably, the fairies were there too and gave us such a warm greeting, it had to be Conan's doing.

Liam and Rory, wearing clinical white coats, talked to the audience about new types of biodegradable plastic being developed and what would happen to the planet if we didn't do something about it. They were well organised with a PowerPoint, and lots of facts and figures.

More photos and appreciation. The fairies were lingering, enjoying the novelty of having four Englishmen in the library. One had been sitting on my lap for a while, as I played the tin whistle. She wore a white and silver dress and a red cloak. Her wings were pink with pale blue tips. All the fairies wore pretty colours and collectively would create a stunning scene. The audience were not able to see them on this occasion. The fairy on my lap suddenly flew up to my ear and whispered; 'Poppy says hello' and was gone. Did she say that? Or was it something else, I wondered? Perhaps it was; 'Now I have to go,' which would fit the context, since she went immediately after. Anyway, I didn't think much of it because the chances of Poppy being in the library in Germany were remote.

Our first full day went extremely well. The next day, officialdom would be involved with a meeting of the Lord Mayor and a journey to the tip, which we all agreed might be somewhat unpleasant.

That evening I had a lot more to tell Lisa and even laughingly told her about my encounter with the fairy who passed on Poppy's greetings.

'As if Poppy would be here. Haven't seen her for years,' I chortled, but Lisa was silent. 'What's up? 'I asked.

'Be careful Don. I love you' was all she said, and hung up.

'That's odd,' I thought. Sleep came quickly and was

strewn with images of what had been; Conan and Poppy, our trip to Allonby, Long Meg and her daughters' stones in rainy Little Selkeld, Steph and the lost year in plastics, Cornwall with Finley and Craggy Jackson, Ballymena, Padraig O'Leary, Ethna O'Flagherty, the bad presence in the Pot of Gold, Toddy's hat, Glastonbury, Gloria, finding Toddy, Grey Land, Bronan, Sol, the black horses, Dad's transformation, my new office, *The Plastic Dragon*, the ridiculous word from the spell and saving the Cotehill branch. Then Conan, but NOT Conan, in my dream I took a longer look at Conan; the groomed beard and combed hair with snazzy clothes were not Conan-like, although the face was his, or was it the face of Bronan? I awoke and sat bolt upright in bed.

'Bronan!' I shouted, expecting Lisa to be beside me, then remembering I was in Germany, where the Grimms had lived.

The phone rang, it was Lisa. 'I'm sorry I hung up, Don. There was no good reason to do that, only that I don't really want our lives to be disrupted again, with the baby coming soon. What if it was Poppy? How does she know you're there?' she said.

'Hmm,' I replied still half asleep. 'It may have something to do with the parcel Conan gave me just before I left. Wants me to pass it on to a cousin of his called Franz. I'd forgotten about it until that moment.'

'Don!' Lisa yelled. 'What have you done? You've landed yourself right back in the middle of something you have nothing to do with. What happens if you finish up in Grey Land and can't get out this time?' She was frantic.

'Don't worry, all will be well. Love you. Must go for breakfast. We meet the Lord Mayor today.' Of course I was worried but didn't want Lisa to suspect that. I probably shouldn't have mentioned the parcel, but it was clear something was going on. Poppy was in Germany, I had a package to give to Franz which contained something I had no clue about, and it was given to me, not by my friend Conan, but by Bronan his dodgy brother from Grey Land and would be collected at some point by a German cousin, Franz. What was going on?

Toddy and the scientists were already at breakfast again, Toddy looked like a pink peppermint with a white and pink stripy suit and yellow shirt. He had a pair of yellow leather shoes on his remarkably long feet. The scientists wore white coats and I had donned jeans and a black t-shirt with the words *Fairies Care About the Planet, So Should We*, in pink.

I wanted to discuss the Bronan situation with Toddy, but couldn't mention it with the scientists present. Althoughthey had entered into the spirit of our trip and were enjoying the stories and history of the place, I was pretty sure they wouldn't readily take the real fairy story on board. I would have to wait until we were alone.

Once in Gretal and ready to hit the road, I checked the glove compartment; the package was still there and I debated whether to leave it or bring it. My instinct was to bring it. If Franz turned up I'd just hand it over and that would be an end to it, but if I left it in the glove compartment, Franz wouldn't bother turning up. I slipped it into my jeans pocket.

The venue for the morning was the Grimm Museum, where we were met by the Lord Mayor, dressed in full regalia. He and the entourage showed us round the museum where we learned a lot more about the remarkable brothers and their stories.

The session was well attended by human folk as well as fairy folk, and there was a great ambience. Toddy and I performed *Sleeping Beauty*; the magic mirror and huge rosy apple we used as props were a great success, and we drew seven children from the audience to play the dwarfs. When I told the Plastic Dragon story, through the interpreter, the children then recited it in German. After the session, we all piled into a bus; the Mayor and his wife, the audience, Toddy, Rory, Liam a photographer and I. We drove through fairy tale country, which had provided so much inspiration for the Grimms, then reached the edge of the province where stoodthe Tip. The Tip was a huge mountain of waste, beside which a crane stood, adding more waste to the top of the mountain. It stood in a giant hole and stank. TV cameras were present, and the Mayor was interviewed about his plans to reduce the size of the tip and the amount of waste, by reducing plastic waste. Rory and Liam were interviewed about the science of it all and gave their message of hope, encouraging producers to choose bio-degradable plastics or other recyclable materials. The children read *The Plastic Dragon* and I was interviewed. The presenter wanted to know what had inspired me to write the story. 'The Cotehill wood fairies.' I replied and immediately regretted it. Toddy threw me a glance, that said; WHAT!

Indeed, what had I done? There was brief silence as it sunk in, and the reporter was straight back on it.

'Feen?' he said. 'Sagen Sie, dass die Feen Sie inspiriert haben?' he repeated. 'Are you saying the fairies inspired you?' my interpreter relayed.

'Die Feen der Cotehill Wälder?' the interpreter turned to me; 'The fairies of Cotehill wood?' I was in a panic. How could I have said it out loud and given my fairies away like that? Images of bus loads of tourists traipsing the woods in search of fairies flashed through my mind.

'Er... in my dreams of course, Not real fairies,' I muttered, but not convincingly. Another nano of silence and the interviewer turned to Toddy.

'Haben Sie schon einmal die Cotehill Feen gesehen Toddy?' he asked, thinking he was onto a great scoop.

'Have I seen a Cotehill fairy?' he said, stalling for time.

'My dear man, I am a Cotehill fairy.'

WHAT?

There was laughter amongst the people and the moment passed. Toddy looked me straight in the eye and I knew he was angry, I also wondered if he meant what he'd just said; Was he really a fairy?

The scientists looked uncomfortable.

On our return to Steinau, there were crowds of cheering people. It seemed that far and wide the eco message was gathering momentum and the folks were rising up to protect what was their right, to enjoy life on a happy planet.

'Don, you've just been on the news,' said Lisa, over the phone, back at the hotel. 'You said the Cotehill fairies inspired you with the Plastic Dragon story.' There are already people traipsing through the woods and it's seven o'clock in the evening.'

I was bereft. 'It slipped out, Lisa. I was caught off guard by the question. I've never regretted anything so much, but I had hoped the impact would have been softened by Toddy's follow up remark,' I said.

'Which was?' Lisa asked.

'He said he's a Cotehill fairy, hahaha.' Lisa was silent. 'Say something Lisa!' We were both on the same page now. Both wondering if it could be true, and if Toddy could *actually* be a fairy.

'I'll phone you later Lisa,' I said grimly, knowing that I was in the thick of it again.

I hung up and wrestled with my thoughts. It could explain Toddy's sudden disappearance and reappearance, his rescuing me with the horses, his great height and huge feet. In fact it was so obviously true, and I hadn't even suspected, not once.

The package was still in my pocket and as yet, no sign of Franz. My thoughts drifted to Poppy. She was in on all this somehow. Why was she in Germany? I began to wonder if I was the butt of a huge fairyland joke. Were they having a good laugh at my expense throughout the realms of the fairy folk? I decided it best to eradicate such thoughts. That way lay madness.

Toddy didn't turn up for dinner that evening and the scientists were obviously keen to avoid any mention of the big revelation of the day. Part of me wanted to say; 'It's true! The fairies are working round the clock to clear up our mess,' but I knew they'd probably catch the next bus home.

I spent the evening in my hotel room reading some literature Lisa had sent with us. It had dawned on me I knew very little about fairies, although I devoted a good part of my life to telling fairy tales. Why were they taboo? Why couldn't I just talk about my encounters to the scientists and discuss their great value in the fight to save the planet we shared? It seemed a great deal had been written about them, many studies undertaken and in-depth examination of the societal structures of groups and individuals within their realms.

The oldest story known is *The Smith and the Devil,* which has been told in thirty-five languages and originated seven thousand years ago, *Little Red Riding Hood*'s origins could be traced a thousand years, *Jack and the Beanstalk*, five thousand years. Scholars, like the Grimms have used the stories to track the spread of the Indo-European language. It seemed to me there was as much science involved in the study as art. I'd met so many elves and fairies now I didn't need convincing, but still was shocked at the prospect of Toddy being a fairy, or more precisely, maybe a giant? Come to think of it, most of his stories were giant related: *Fin McCool, The Selfish Giant, Jack the Giant Killer, The Gentle Giant* …

So Toddy was a giant. I concluded.

Lisa phoned. 'There are people all over the woods, Don. Hundreds of them with tents and torches, planning to camp out and look for the fairies,' she said. This was disturbing news. They were not likely to glimpse fairies, but they could destroy their habitat.

'They're wearing your *Fairies Care About the Planet, So Should We* t-shirts.'

I thought this was great but didn't say so. 'What will I do?' she asked.

'Call Mum and Dad and make tea for them,' I replied out of desperation.

'Make tea for your Mum and Dad?' Lisa replied, sounding puzzled.

'No, for the people,' I said. She slammed the phone down before I told her about Toddy being a giant.

I fell asleep and in my dreams fairies paraded before me in their thousands, flying in and out of my vision, all colours and sizes from tiny to giant, elves, pixies, piskies, leprechauns, gnomes, there were unicorns and brownies. Brownies, I thought in my dream state. Conan's a brownie. Where are you, Conan?

I awoke and felt afraid and in danger. The dream was disturbing and I suddenly felt out of my depth. Why was I here in Grimm's land, with a giant and a strange package? Where was Franz and where were Conan and Poppy? I should be home with my Lisa and my woods. Instead, I had caused havoc in the woods and Lisa had to deal with it. I destroyed her peace.

I decided to go home immediately. I'd leave the package at hotel reception for Toddy the giant. He was a fairy, he'd know what to do with it.

I packed my bag. It was dawn, and I thought there would be a train out of there soon, so left the package and a note and headed out. I'd travel overland, I thought, and reach home in two days. At the station, I found there was an hour to wait for the first train, so settled on a bench and breathed in the fresh morning air. I thought about home and Lisa and our baby on the way. This fairy nonsense had no place in our lives. I watched the day unfold at the station. The ticket office open up and early birds arriving for the trains. I thought about the brothers Grimm and their lives in these parts, how hard their lives became when their father died and how they struggled to make ends meet, and yet they carried on pursuing their dream, engrossed in their pursuit of stories and ambition to leave a legacy worth leaving. They didn't give up. And then I thought about our tour and all the venues Simon booked and the people waiting along the route to see us and hear our stories and the message for our planet that many people care about. I thought about the Cotehill fairies labouring away as they had been for so long before I stumbled on them, trying to clean up the mess, and the other fairies who had cheered me on and brightened up my life by coming to the gigs in appreciation for joining them in their battle for our planet.

'Don't give up.' I heard a tiny voice in my ear, as clear as the day I was sitting in, it said; 'Don't give up.' And so I returned to the hotel.

Toddy and the scientists were at breakfast when I arrived and were surprised to see me with my luggage arriving at the hotel. Eyebrows were collectively raised. Breakfast was brief as we had to set off for the next stage of our journey. We secured the luggage to the roof, piled into Gretel and set off along the fairy tale trail. I was still deep in my thoughts about the events of the day before, and my dream, but the voice had clearly told me not to give up.

Rory had devised a quiz to keep us entertained along the way and asked questions on the theme of our journey.Toddy had lined up some German rock tunes on a cassette tape and Tangerine Dream, an old sixties band, lifted our spirits as we drove along the fairy trail.

'Thanks for the gift, Don,' Toddy said. I initiated a swift search of the memory files, but came up with no recollection of giving Toddy a gift, so searched again because he had obviously received one. 'Is it authentic?' he asked. 'I mean, if it is, it must be worth a lot of money. Are you sure you want me to have it? Interesting coin though, never seen one like it. It puzzled me when the hotel receptionist gave me the package, but I now gather you had left. Is everything OK at home?' Where to begin...

Chapter 31

Toddy Disappears

The scientists were up front. Liam was driving, and they were listening to Tangerine Dream, so I could talk to Toddy without them hearing.

'This is a long story, Toddy,' I began.

'OK, give me the short version,' he said.

'Right, short version. Just before we left, who I thought was Conan, but now think was Bronan, gave me a package to give to his cousin Franz when I arrived in Germany. So far Franz hasn't turned up. Poppy the fairy is in Germany and there are people camping in Cotehill woods looking for fairies. I'm worried about Lisa and our baby yet to be born. And also Toddy... I've figured you out.' I added, deciding to go for it. He looked surprised at this.

'Figured me out? What's that supposed to mean?' he said indignantly.

'It means I know you're a fairy. The giant sort. You're a giant, Toddy. Don't deny it. You admitted it yourself.'

He laughed, quietly, at first, then louder and louder and more and more out of control until tears rolled down his cheeks, whereupon we arrived at Alsfeld. Rory had the map and hotel address and within no time at all we'd checked in.

'We need to talk, Don,' Toddy said as he set off for the lift to his room. 'Let's meet in the lobby in half an hour.'

Alsfeld is a quaint town where the house of Little Red Riding Hood stands. It is an enchanting town, with half-timbered houses, and is close to Hesse, where the brothers were born. My hotel had a balcony overlooking the square. I unpacked, showered and was ready to meet Toddy in good time. In the lobby I watched tourists come and go. Suitcases full of stuff appeared and disappeared. Weary travellers arrived, refreshed travellers left. Different nationalities, cultures and languages met in the lobby and dispersed. I sat contemplating, until I checked my watch and realised I'd been there an hour and there was no sign of Toddy.

I asked reception to call his room but there was no response. I called his mobile, but there was no response. I waited longer and thought about the package that I now knew held a coin. I thought about Toddy's response when I said he was a giant. He had laughed, but hadn't denied it. His parting words; 'We need to talk' were promising, but he hadn't turned up. What was going on? My phone rang, and it was Rory to say he, Liam and Toddy had gone looking for a coffee shop, and Toddy fell down a hole in the high street. It was a disused well covered by a loose paving slab. The police and ambulance were on the spot and they couldn't get a response when they rang his phone. Shocked, I got the location and ran to find the place. It was easy to locate as there were police, flashing lights and an ambulance at the scene. They let me through once they'd established who I was and that I knew the man in the well.

'How deep is it?' I asked a policeman, but he didn't understand. 'Ich spreche kein Englisch,' he said. Liam and Rory also could not establish the depth of the well.

'One minute we were talking and laughing, the next he'd gone,' said Liam. 'We looked all around us and then we looked down and saw the hole. There's no other explanation, he must be down there,' he added.

'So you didn't actually see him fall in?' I asked.

'No,' Rory replied, 'but it's the only logical conclusion.' So spoke the scientist. However, I had my doubts.

The rescue operation continued and night fell. There was still no response from Toddy. I had contacted Simon to let him know, and the police arranged for a translator to join us. It seemed the well was about thirty feet deep and there may be water at the bottom. Finally firemen arrived at the scene with a long rope ladder, which they secured to the top of the well and let it roll down. One brave man climbed in and began the descent. We waited around at the top feeling helpless and imagining poor Toddy down there and what state he could be in. He could be dead, or injured. Either way, it wasn't looking good for the tour. An hour passed. There had been no movement on the rope for fifteen minutes, and everyone was anxious, not only for Toddy, but for the poor guy who'd gone down there looking for him, whose radio was dead, much to the frustration of his colleagues. Finally, the rope ladder moved and there was audible relief. For another ten minutes we waited, not knowing what to expect, and then the fireman appeared and pulled himself up to the top of the well. Strapped to his back was Toddy, apparently lifeless. They rushed him to hospital, with us following behind in a police car. I rang Simon to fill him in on events and suggested he let Mary, Toddy's wife know as soon as possible.

    He lay unconscious for two days in a bed he didn't fit, and his wife Mary arrived to be by his side. We didn't think he'd pull through, but just as we were about to leave the hospital on the second day, he opened his eyes and spoke.

    'Mary my love, what are you doing here?'

    The rest of the tour was cancelled, and the newspapers were very sympathetic. We planned for Toddy to return home for treatment of his broken leg. He would fly back with Mary and the scientists and I would drive home in Gretel.

    All was packed and ready to go on the final night of our stay, and I was at my hotel window looking down on the square and all the activities going on there, when a little voice said;

    'Hello, Don, I'm Franz, Conan's cousin. I believe you have a package for me.'

    The little man was very crooked and pointy; pointy nose, ears fingers and feet. He wore a red hat and his beard was long and white.

    I held my head in my hands for a while, exasperated. 'I haven't got your package, Franz' I said, deciding not to beat about the bush. 'But just a moment.' I rang Toddy, who was still in hospital. 'How are you Toddy? I enquired politely. I have Franz here, he wants his parcel.' There was a pause, then Toddy replied.

    'Don, I haven't got it any more. I think it may be down the well.'

    That was all I needed! I relayed the message to Franz.

    'He hasn't got the package any more, Franz. It may be at the bottom of a well.'

Franz made a strange noise and I couldn't make out what he said. It didn't sound very nice though.

'Look Franz, none of this has anything to do with me. I know nothing about a package of yours, I'm only the messenger, and there has been a series of unfortunate events which prevented me from handing the infernal thing over to you. Why did you arrive so late? I expected you days ago!'

'Well, Don boy, here's the deal. Without that package, you'll never see your old friends Conan or Poppy again.' I was beaten.

'And how, cousin Franz, can that be?' I responded, with an equal measure of sarcasm.

'Sit down Don.'

'Jumping Jehoshaphat!' I cried, channelling Dad. Then I sat down in the comfy hotel armchair, ready to hear another story.

'For reasons I can't explain, because of top secrecy, a branch of the Cotehill fairies moved to Germany two hundred years ago, your time. They had to depart in haste and left behind a lot of treasure in the Fairy Queen's care. We are not greedy folk and can live humbly, but we have a greedy dragon who must be fed gold every one hundred years. The Fairy Queen has been true to her word and sent gold every century with a little extra for this and that. This time, however, she seemed to have forgotten and despite our requests, she didn't send it. She said we have used the treasure up. So cutting a long story short.'

'You're holding Poppy and Conan to ransom' I interrupted.

'In short, yes.' He said. 'They're in no danger and living in comfort with their German cousins, but without the gold they can never return to Cotehill woods.'

'So tell me, Franz,' I ventured, 'who gave me the package?'

'That would be cousin Bronan, Conan's brother. Another spin off from this deal, if it goes through, is that Bronan will be released from Grey Land and returned to his family home, because he will have helped some-one.'

'I see,' I said wearily. 'As I said, Franz, the package is down the well.'

'Show me the well.' he said impatiently. He sat on my

shoulder muttering while I took him to the place where the well was. Once there, he studied it and tried to move the paving slab, which was now fixed properly over the top.

'This will require some brute strength,' he concluded and, with a snap of his fingers, summoned up an ogre who soon removed the stone, and Franz flew down the well with two fairies to light the way. If only life was as simple for humans, I thought.

After a short while, he re-appeared with the gold coin and the ogre replaced the stone, making sure no one could fall into the well again. Franz and his companions were happy, and I went back to the hotel to sleep. I phoned Lisa before I dropped off, and told her that Franz had the coin and Conan and Poppy had been held ransom in Germany, but would now be released.

How were things in the woods? It seemed Dad had erected a tea and coffee stall and was selling Plastic Dragon t-shirts to raise funds for eco projects. The council had been round to check on safety and erected temporary toilet booths. Children were having a great time looking for fairies, and Lisa and her friends were holding storytelling sessions in the woods. Also, the Shakespeare Theatre Company had been in touch to ask if they could perform *A Midsummer Night's Dream*.

Chapter 32

The Homecoming

The scientists and I set off early next morning and trusty Gretel, carried us through the lovely towns and hamlets of Germany, back to the Hook of Holland and the ferry. We had a good journey listening to the tapes Toddy left for us and talking about future projects in the factory. I wanted to discuss the Conan affair with them and speculate on his and Poppy's return. What if the cousins didn't release Poppy and Conan? What if they kept them there and held them ransom forever? I didn't think that would happen. Franz seemed a decent sort. He was just trying to save his folks.

    The ferry crossing was a little rocky but the sky was clear and a blue moon shone down on the inky water, laying a path for the ferry to follow. We went to the restaurant for fish, chips and mushy peas with a cup of tea. There was a singer crooning a Frank Sinatra song *My Way*, and a few people dancing. I finished my meal and left the scientists to it. I needed sleep. The cabin was miniscule, but I was only interested in the bed and fell on it. The boat rocked, and I soon drifted off to sleep.

    My dreams were filled with images of Lisa at the library, on her bike, shivering at Meg and her daughter's stones in the rain, at Watts coffee shop, our wedding, her long black hair always silky smooth and shiny, her dark eyes as deep and dark as the waves upon which we sailed. I awoke with these gentle memories on my mind. She was my very own Lisa and I never wanted to be apart from her again. I decided that if ever I was to tour in the future, she and our baby would come with me.

Dawn broke, and I went out on deck to see the land ahead and watch as we drifted towards the coast. Liam and Rory joined me on deck and were feeling rough after making a night of it in the bar and on the dance floor. I'd really warmed to them. Never thought I'd get on with a scientist, but now I had two scientist friends.

I had tried to prepare myself for the scene in the wood, tried to visualise how it would be from what Lisa had told me, but even then I was shocked as Gretel pulled into the village. Cotehill was a hub for visitors coming and going from the woods. There were stalls lining the pavements and selling crafts, fairy ornaments, trees, Plastic Dragon t-shirts, pottery replicas of Toddy's camper van... you name it they had it. The stalls stretched all the way into the woods until the little stile that led to the lake. I climbed the stile and there were people everywhere in my lovely, peaceful wood. They were picnicking, climbing trees, they had spy glasses and were combing the ground for fairies, trampling the wildlife. I reached my cottage and found a tea stall set up outside with Mum and Dad at the helm. There were plates of scones, chocolate brownies, banana cake and Mum's famous quiche. They had placed several tables in the garden and folk were chatting and studying maps which Lisa had drawn up of the wood. Just beyond the garden gate stood a bright yellow tent inside which was Toddy, with his leg plastered and propped on a chair. Gathered around him, children intently listened to the story of the Cotehill fairies.

Lisa was inside the cottage, preparing sandwiches and I surprised her.

'Don! You're home.' She beamed and looked so happy, I had to contain my true feelings. How I wanted my wood back. I didn't want to share it with all these people. I wanted the peace I'd always found there. Instead, I had returned to a rural Disney Land.

'Don, it's been so exciting while you were gone.' Lisa went on. 'Ever since the news showed your interview. And the papers latched on to it, Cotehill has become a huge attraction. People are getting rich because of it. Stan will turn one of his fields into a car park because the village can't cope with all the traffic. I think I must leave my library post and devote myself to the fairy business full-time. There's so much potential, Don.

We can build our own fairy library next to the cottage and some fairy tale structures in the woods. A little Red Riding Hood house, a Rapunzel tower, that sort of thing.' I listened, waiting to wake up, but that didn't happen.

While I was inside the cottage, word got round that I'd returned and it shocked me to open my front door and find a huge banner toting crowd shouting; 'Kill the plastic dragon!' and calling for a speech. I looked beyond the crowd to where the fairy line was every night and almost cried. I was wishing with all my heart that they were OK, and all of this had not destroyed their lives, it was my fault. I should never have told the reporter in Germany that the Cotehill fairies had inspired me. It had caused the beginning of the end for the branch I had tried so hard to save by finding Toddy and the lost word.

I spoke a few words to the crowd and thanked them for their support, then walked away, into the woods. I needed to think. But the woods were not the same woods I had left behind. They were populated now. I walked the furthest I could until I finally found a quiet space, where I rested on a log. I'd had a long journey back from Grimm land and needed time and space to put my thoughts in order.

Tomorrow I'd return to work, and now that I'd spent time with the scientists I knew more about what we needed for the future, and wanted to make our factory the most innovative eco factory in the world. That must not be an impossible dream. It was the most important thing I must do, and intended to make sure the scientists had everything they needed to fulfil the vision.

As regards fairyland I presumed all was well now, although some feedback from the enigmatic Conan and Poppy would be appreciated. And was Toddy a fairy giant?

'Don! Don!' someone called. I looked around me, but saw no-one. 'Don!' I heard again.

'Hello?' I replied and waited. 'Hello?' But there was no response. Making my way back to the tourist hub that my living space had become, I searched for the person who had called me. I recognised the voice, but couldn't place the owner. It was a familiar voice, a familiar call, but I couldn't remember who.

Toddy had finished his story telling session when I arrived back at the cottage. I pushed his wheelchair into the village and we called in at the Greyhound.

'Don and Toddy! Our heroes!' Gale, the landlady gushed, leaving her post behind the bar to greet us. 'We've never done such good business, thanks to you two. That fairy yarn's a gudun!' she laughed. 'Mind you, the plastic message is getting through and that's the main thing. What can I get you? It's on the house!'

At last I had Toddy alone and I could interrogate him.

'Are you a fairy giant, Toddy?' I asked.

'Well, Don it depends what you mean by fairy giant. As you can see, I am a giant, or could be construed as a giant, being almost seven feet tall. I have also had dealings with the fairies, but I'm not a born fairy. I think the term is, touched by fairies.' He sipped his beer. 'Yes, I'd say I've been touched by the fairies, and a little of their magic has rubbed off on me. Also, I will do anything within my means to protect our fairy friends, as I know would you, Don. You are a great protector of the fairy realm.'

That was true. I would. I wondered if fairies had touched me.

'Not as such, Don. You have no magic. They have given me a little magic power, because they trust me and can send me on missions, like the one to rescue you from Grey Land. They can give me a little power like that, but it's a short-term thing. Not made to last. There are a few humans like that. I can't name them all, but your granny Indigo and great, great granddad Seth were two of them I know of.' This startled me, although why anything could ever startle me again, I'll never know. I tried to recall Granny and any clues to tell me she had special powers. As I said Don, the powers are temporary, short term.'

I met Mum and Dad at their gate, just as they pulled up, having left the tea stall for the evening. They looked so happy together, carrying plates and bags full of food. I helped them with the stuff and went inside.

'Don, we're having the time of our lives up there in the woods,' said Mum, stashingfood in the fridge. 'It's been so much fun and really brought the village folk together.' I'd never seen her so animated before.

'I've been thinking a lot recently, Donovan,' Dad said.'The factory's getting too much for me now. I'm happy running the tea stall in the wood and you're doing great things in the plastic world. I couldn't be more proud of you. I want you to run the show. You can have my office, do whatever you like with it. I trust you. Your Mum and I will develop the tea stall. We have ideas.'

Mum sensed my concern.

'Nothing distasteful Donovan. It will be an eco-friendly place. We want to promote your idea and act on it. Everything will be recyclable and locally grown where possible. Tea and coffee can't be locally grown, but we can make sure no humans or fairies have been harmed anywhere along the production line.' They impressed me. They had done their research and a fraction of me was warming to the transformation.

The sun was low in the sky as I walked home along the familiar country lanes, lined with bright white umbellifers and purple rosebay willow herb. The hedgerows were alive with chaffinches and hawthorn flowers, and beyond the hedgerows lay fields strewn with sheep and cows. The fields gently rose to form distant hills clad in summer crops.

The woods were quiet now. At the cottage. Lisa was tidying up after the busy day of baking and overseeing events. She too glowed with the same aura I'd seen in my parents.

'I was sceptical at first Don, but it seems right. The people are coming to support your ideas. They are coming together because they want to be part of it and help. There's so much potential for community spirit. And your folks and mine are right behind it. I understand it's hard to have to share your woods with others, but they were never solely ours, they belong to everyone and as long as the people are coming in good faith and not coming to destroy what is here, then surely it's a good thing. Kids from the city learning about trees and listening to fairy stories. People enjoying life in an eco-friendly environment, Can't be a bad thing, can it?'

I could see her point. Lisa was so eloquent and passionate, I could see that my reaction was born of selfishness, and we should share the woods and all they offered.

We dined at the long table which had remained since our wedding. Lisa had prepared a lasagne with salad and baked an apple pie for my homecoming. After, I took her to see the fairy line glowing as it always did, and the fairies still working at extracting the rubbish from our planet. Lisa cried when she saw them relentlessly passing the old plastic parts from one to the other in a never-ending motion, like it would continue for eternity.

'Now I understand,' she said, tears streaming down her cheeks. 'I know why you're doing it and I'll always do everything in my power to protect the fairy habitat.'

We stood a while and watched. Your mum and I.

Chapter 33

Three Wishes

Early the next morning I went for a walk, wanting to experience my wood, before the tourists arrived. I walked in the direction Conan had taken to show Toddy and me the fairyland tree. The grass glistened with dew and there was a wonderful earthy aroma of wild garlic, while insects hummed, birds sang and a woodpecker hammered away somewhere up a tall tree. I walked until the last oak tree and then beyond and into the place I didn't recognise as my wood.

'You made it, Don boy.' The familiar voice came from behind me. 'You found your way here at last.' I smiled when I saw him for the first time in a while, with his tangle of red hair and straggly beard, Conan was back and there beside him stood Poppy and Bronan. Three tiny beings who'd made a big impact on my life.

'Come over and sit with us at the tree,' Conan said, and we all settled down around the ancient oak. 'First, we've got to thank you for saving the tree and getting me and Bronan back together,' said Conan.

'I've changed, Don,' Bronan assured me. 'I'm no longer that man you met in Grey Land, thanks to you. If you hadn't given the gold coin to Franz, I'd have still been there and Conan and Poppy would be in Germany instead of here where they belong, with the Cotehill branch. I'm loving being back!' he said. A changed man.

'What about Sol?' I asked. I'd often thought about sad Sol and the miserable existence he led there in that awful place.

'Sol's OK' said Bronan. 'I set him free, and he's doing

his own thing somewhere in the Caribbean.' That sounded positive.

'And Don,' Poppy joined in. 'It was so brave of you to go off in search of Toddy Oggy. I know you had some scary moments, especially at the Pot of Gold in Ballymena, where that evil imp almost took the word from you. He knew the words were in the hat, but you acted so swiftly; he had no chance to get to you and then Conan and I organised a tunnel of protection along the road to get you safely home.'

I remembered it all, but hearing it from their point of view made sense of everything, especially the bad imp in Ireland. I was right to run away.

'The fairy realm owe you a debt of gratitude Don,' Conan beamed, 'and would like to grant you three wishes. You have time to think about them. Just say them out loud when you decide.' I immediately forgot about this offer.

We talked for a while longer about the brothers Grimm and life in Germany. Had a laugh about Toddy falling down the well, and me thinking he was a fairy, and then came round to what was happening in the wood.

'Don't worry Don boy, we've got a handle on it. We'll make sure no harm comes to any trees or fairy habitats, but we think it's a great thing to get the folks away from their TVs and into the woods. It will be fine.'

Feeling reassured by that and thrilled to have seen my old friends again, I headed back to the last oak tree, or the first oak tree, depending how you looked at it.

Back at the cottage, Lisa and I had breakfast in the garden. The honeysuckle was in full bloom around the front door and draped over the gateway. Its perfume was intoxicating. We feasted on yogurt and honey, with crumpets and a pot of coffee, and talked about our plans. You would soon join us Fionuala, and we needed to make a space for you. The question was, should it be in the town house or the country house? We decided on both. And so began choosing the colours. We didn't know if you were a boy or girl at that stage, so we went for neutral.

At work I moved into Dad's office and ordered more plants of all sizes and species to liven it up.

Some grim figures were coming out from the scientists' research, which showed that whatever we were doing and however long we tried, it seemed we would never get a handle on the plastic waste problem.

I called in on Liam and Rory to find out what was going on. They showed me the facts and figures, and they were worrying. 'I wish we had more money to throw at this,' I said. (wish number one) 'We could do with a multinational approach. From the response we got in Germany, we're not alone in this.'

The scientists agreed. Money and determination and top level scientists were key to finding a lasting solution to the plastic problem.

I spent my day writing emails to MPs, supermarket chain managers, fast-food outlets and anyone else I could think of who needed to know what lay ahead if things didn't change. Later, I turned my thoughts to the storytelling gig at the Blue Moon on Wednesday. *The Plastic Dragon* was doing well, but the campaign needed a new boost.

Toddy phoned during the day and asked me to call in to his house later. I agreed to go on my way home. Toddy and Mary lived in a house on the edge of Cotehill. Surrounded by fields, it resembled a ship sailing on a green sea. It was a sturdy house with deep bay windows each side of the front door.

Toddy and Mary were waiting for me when I arrived on Ivanhoe, greeting me warmly and ushered me inside. The interior flouted convention; they had painted the walls every imaginable colour and there were murals depicting scenes and characters taken from fairy tales. The ceilings were high to accommodate Toddy's great height, and in every nook and cranny there were books and treasures reflecting their great love of literature.

'Thanks for coming, Don. Good to see you. I'll get straight to the point. Mary and I have money problems. Since falling down the well I haven't been out and about making money and the debts are piling up.' Toddy was still in the wheelchair. It seemed so unfair that he should be in that situation, he wasn't young like me.

'We will sell the house and move into Gretel.' This took me by surprise. How would they live in Gretel? She was ideal for travelling across Europe but not for *living* in. I felt very sad as I left them.

'I wish there was a pot of gold I could give you, Toddy, (wish number two) but we have the baby coming now and we've invested a lot of money in the business.'

'Don! We expect nothing from you. Just wanted to let you know. We'll put the house up for sale next week.'

I travelled home slowly through the woods on Ivanhoe, feeling very down. It had not been a good day what with the news from the scientists and now Toddy's news. There was a chill in the air which made me shudder, and the trees cast malevolent shadows, or perhaps I imagined them. Nature reflecting my mood.

Lisa had cooked her speciality, shepherd's pie, which lifted my spirits somewhat, and I went out to chop wood. We needed to replenish the woodpile before winter crept in. There was a thicket just up the slope behind the cottage where I kept the wood block and hand-saw in a small shed. I made my way there and set to work. Absorbed in the task, I was disturbed by the voice again.

'Don! Don!' it called, and I looked all around me, but there was no-one in sight. I went back to work thinking it was a trick of the wind amongst the trees, but it happened again.

'Donovan! Donovan!' Now I was spooked and was about to take off when Dad appeared up the slope. I was confused, but relieved.

'Your Mum and I have just called in to see how things are going. Is all well?' He was a little out of breath, I noticed, unusual for him. I told him about my fears for the plastic campaign. And that what we were doing was a tiny speck compared to what needed to be done.

He and Mum stayed a while and admired the paintwork in the nursery and the murals Toddy had helped Lisa to draw on the walls.

'All it needs is the cradle,' Mum said, and we all nodded and smiled, imagining the cradle and the child soon to be born, asleep in it.

We had decided the woods would only open to the public at weekends, which was working out well for all concerned. The craft makers had time to prepare their wares, the woods had time to recover, and we had our peace back.

I returned to the job of chopping wood, contemplating the little crib we would get for our baby, when again I heard the voice.

'Don! Over here, Don!' I knew the voice it was so familiar, but still couldn't put a name to it. I decided to wander around in the direction it seemed to emanate.

'Here!' And there she was, my granny Indigo, exactly as I remembered her in her floral dress and green shawl and smiling with such radiance. She stood a few feet away and looking to her left she beckoned, and from the shadow of the trees came a small man carrying a cradle. He placed it on the ground in front of Granny and stood beside her, and then I realised it was Great, Great Granddad Seth, who had made all the furniture in the house.

He had made you a cradle.

They stood for a while, watching. I didn't want to move in case they left, so I sent a text to Lisa telling her to come outside quickly. She ran to my side expecting an injury, but followed my gaze and saw Seth and Indigo and the cradle. I said 'thank you!' and they waved and disappeared, leaving behind the most exquisite cradle any baby would wish to sleep in. We carried it into the house and placed it in the designated space to await its designated occupant.

The next day at work I received an email from the local MP to say he would bring up my plastic concerns in the next Prime Minister's Question Time meeting scheduled for Wednesday. He shared my concern and believed the problem should be funded at the highest level. I phoned Lisa immediately with the news, but was side-tracked because she had gone into labour five minutes earlier.

That day was such a confusion of events; rushing home, rushing to the hospital, phoning and messaging all and sundry, waiting and waiting until you arrived. Our baby girl was with us at last. There was a flurry of celebrations and excitement until finally we all came home together and two became three in our little cottage.

Toddy, Mary, Simon and our folks were there to greet us as we pulled up outside the cottage, and there was a pile of pink blankets, bootees and matinee jackets in the crib.

You were a beauty, we all agreed.

Chapter 34

The Last Oak Tree

Later that week I had a call from the MP to say he'd brought the plastic question up, and that the Prime Minister had shown genuine concern and would ensure the provision of funds and research into dealing with the impact of plastics on future generations. I was astounded, but appreciative.

'Let's see if they can put their money where their mouths are,' said Dad. However, true to their word funds were provided and scholarships created for science students to tackle the issue.

At the weekend Toddy set up his story tent and called in to see me. 'Just came to tell you the good news, Don. It seems the landlord of The Pot of Gold in Ballymena has died and left the pub to me in his will. He was a good friend of mine and loved the stories. Seems he wants to make sure the story-telling tradition is kept alive, and the best way he could think of for doing that was through leaving the place to me. We'll be going over there next week to sort things out.

'That's amazing Toddy!' I said. It really was good news, but it would be sad to see him go and I told him so.

'We won't stay there, Don. I thought we could keep the place rolling and find a manager to book the gigs for a while at least. If it works out, we can make some profit and keep the house here. All depends what happens when we go next week.'

The universe seemed to be on a role, two good things in one day.

Wednesdays at the Blue Moon continued and Simon kept the momentum going for the Plastic Dragon campaign, but I knew we needed some new input and rummaged around my brain for an idea that would take off. Finally it came to me and I wrote the story.

The Last Oak Tree

Once upon a time there was an oak tree that grew on the edge of an old wood in England. It was the last oak tree before fairyland. The elves, goblins, brownies and fairies always knew their way back to fairyland, because the last oak tree in the wood had been standing there for centuries, since the days of King Arthur, it had seen witches and wizards passing to and from between the world of humans and the world of fairy.

Its branches spread like welcoming arms, and it was a wise old tree.

One day some men visited the woods with red chalk and chalked an X on many of the trees. And the next day they came with axes and saws and chopped them down. Then they brought big machines and cement and flattened the ground where the wood had been, then poured on the cement so that the trees could never grow back. The last oak tree was still standing, but they broke its heart. The wood was now a car-park, and all the lovely sights and sounds the oak tree knew were gone. The birds and butterflies, the bluebells in spring and wild roses in summer, the hawthorn and beech and sycamore trees were no more. When it rained, the rain could not get through and the last oak tree's roots were parched. The fairies were deeply saddened that the wood had gone and would comfort the tree every night and day until one summer no buds appeared on his branches. The last oak tree died of grief.

The fairies were so saddened by this that they moved away.

So now the dead oak tree marks the entrance to a giant supermarket, and there is nothing left of the beautiful wood that once stood in its place.

I debut the story that week with music and some lighting

effects. The fairies were there and I could see them weeping at the thought of what could happen, and what was happening all over the country as they cleared woods to make way for progress. *The Last Oak Tree* story became a great success and *The Plastic Dragon* publishers snapped it up. The illustrations, were spectacular and captured the beauty and fragility of our woodlands and the life within them.

The wood weekends continued to draw the public and now I was able to include *The Last Oak Tree* in the tour. Small wooden structures would now and then appear around the woods, miniature cottages and palaces with the exquisite craftsmanship of which only Seth was capable.

Toddy was still in Ireland but would be back in time for the next Blue Moon meeting.

You enthralled your Mum and me, and you joined us on our woodland walks as you grew. I kept the promise I'd made to myself after the Grimm trip, that I would never tour without you and your mum. It wasn't so bad since Lisa had given up work in the library to take care of the woodland library she had created and, being the boss, I could take time off whenever I deemed it necessary and any tour that involved saving the planet spreading news, was necessary. So Simon booked a few tours.

One day Toddy phoned me; 'Don! If you get a letter in the post, don't open it whatever you do!' and hung up.

Lisa and I planned the tours Simon had booked. Starting early September, we always enjoyed creating the programme for each venue; Northumberland would be dragon themed, inspired by the story of Margaret, turned into a dragon by her wicked jealous stepmother Behoc, and can only be saved by three kisses. In Nottingham we planned a Robin Hood event, Yorkshire; a theme of Knights and castles, Warwickshire; The Forbidden Forest, and so on and so forth. We made some notes for the artist we had found to help with the scenery. *The Plastic Dragon* and *The Last Oak Tree* would travel everywhere with us.

One evening there was a knock at the door. It was Mum, and she looked unhappy. She came to let us know that Dad was very sick. I went to get my jacket.

'No need to come right away Donovan, he's at home but has a serious lung problem, The doctors will try to treat it, but don't know if he will survive or not. They say he has a fifty-fifty chance.' My stomach lurched. I'd never known Dad to have a day off work. He had never been sick, and to be faced with this was horrendous. It would explain his breathlessness when he called to see me while I was chopping wood.

    Mum left after a while and we promised to call in early next morning. It seemed Dad would have to go into hospital on Friday for an operation on Monday morning. So soon! After the operation we'd have a clearer prognosis. Mum was devastated but brave. I couldn't imagine life without Dad around, even though we'd had our differences over the years, I'd always loved and admired him.

    'Don, try not to think the worst,' Lisa said, and held my hand. We sat for a long time in silence. The spectre of death looming over us. Something we had never needed to confront before.

    'I just can't imagine how Mum would fare without him, Lisa. He's been her rock.'

    'Don boy,' the familiar voice I hadn't heard for so long came out of the blue as usual. Conan was sitting in his favourite place on the mantelpiece beside Seth's picture.

    'Don, we've got this one. Don't worry. As long as I'm around I'll not let anything bad happen to your dad. Trust me. Beautiful daughter by the way.' He jumped down from the mantelpiece and stroked your head, smiling gently and gazing at your sleeping face as if you were the loveliest thing on the planet, which you are.

Chapter 35

Conan's Promise

We called at Mum and Dad's place early next day. Dad didn't look well and was propped up with pillows on the couch.

'Donovan,' his voice was weak and hoarse. 'Donovan. I'm going to be fine, don't worry. But if I'm not, I want you to look after your mother. She'll be well provided for and you'll have the factory.' He paused for a while. 'Just remember to stand by your eco principals. You're doing a great job.' He stopped talking. It was obviously a big effort.

'You need to rest, Dad and don't worry, you'll be fine,' I said, clinging to Conan's promise.

Dad went into hospital the next day, Friday, and the weekend passed in a subdued manner. People came to the woods as usual but it was hard to have much enthusiasm about the event. Toddy was away, so I stood in for his story tent, and Lisa and Mum provided the refreshments as usual. Some people camped out, and we built the bonfire and sang songs. It took our minds off Dad's sickness, but I couldn't feel the joy I usually felt. I lay awake that night with Dad in my thoughts and how hard he'd worked all his life. He'd always had energy and enthusiasm for everything he did, I smiled as I recalled how strongly I'd opposed his factory and all he stood for, not knowing he was caught in a spell. Who would have thought it? And how he always told me to get my hair cut. I'd grown up a lot since those days, and now we were on exactly the same page. I wasn't ready to lose him yet. There was so much we could still do together, and he had his lovely granddaughter to watch as she grew. The weekend passed in this way, thoughts of loss making you realise what you have.

We visited Dad in hospital and Simon came along with fruit and flowers. He was a good sort.

We invited Simon back to the cottage for a bite of supper and to talk about the plans we already had in place for the tour. I had been thinking hard about whether to show him the fairy line. The fairies may not want him to see them, in which case they wouldn't show, but he had helped to create our success and I'd often thought he should be in on it more deeply. After supper I walked him through the wood and pointed to the line of light ahead. He saw it, so I carried on, until we stood beside it and he watched, stunned.

'This was my inspiration, Simon' I told him. 'I meant what I said at the interview in Germany. My inspiration came from the Cotehill fairies.' He watched their relentless motion as they pulled the plastic from some invisible pile and disposed of it into an invisible void.

We stood in silence for at least ten minutes. Finally he spoke. 'It explains the hat thing and the fairies at your gigs,' he said.

'You see them?' It was my turn to be surprised.

'All the time. I thought you didn't,' Simon answered. Despite my worry over Dad, I had to laugh about that. All that time Simon had been seeing the fairies and not let on. I wondered how many more people that applied to. Maybe there was a problem with Conan's forget-you-ever-saw-it spell.

~

Meanwhile, you, our beautiful daughter, were a delight to behold. Every day you grew a little more and from the tiny, fragile bundle we'd brought home with us that summer's day. By autumn you had smiled, the most enchanting smile imaginable. Your eyes were the same deep brown as your mum's, and you had her shiny black hair. Each day we marvelled at you as you slept in Great, Great Granddad Seth's gift to you, the cradle. Your grandparents would come and coo over you, besotted. You had made our happy lives complete, turned our story into a fairy tale and, of course you were touched by fairy. I was there when Conan gently lay his hand on your head. I saw the moment it brought all the Cotehill fairy branch to our cottage. They came especially for you, and for the first time, I saw the Fairy Queen of Cotehill. She flew to your cradle; she wore a crown and had long, auburn tresses. She had a translucent gown of aquamarine and carried a wand of gold. You stirred in your sleep and opened those big brown eyes. She hovered over you and the whole of fairyland sang in beautiful harmony. You smiled your most enchanting smile and the fairy queen touched your forehead with her wand. For a moment everything went quiet and still. It was a magic moment. Then the queen turned to me and smiled the most radiant smile imaginable and flew away, followed by her subjects, leaving Conan and I in the room gazing at you.

'She is a magical child, Don boy,' Conan said. Then he was gone. The cuckoo clock told me it was eight o'clock on the eighth day of August 1998, and you were eight months old. I left you to sleep and went downstairs to where your Mother was working at our old treadle sewing machine. She was making felt pictures of *The Last Oak Tree,* decorated with a border of acorns. I sat in the old big chair and listened to the rhythm of the treadle as the sun went down.

There were times I'd recall all the mad things that had happened since Conan turned up in my life and how he'd turned a hum-drum would be story telling young hopeful into a man who had lived his own fairy tale, visited places where stories were told, written and inspired, been captured by a brownie, held prisoner in a grey castle, carried magical packages to save the German branch of fairyland, been inspired to do something to help save the planet, by the wonderful hard-working fairies of Cotehill, heard stories of Conan in the past and his friendship with Indigo and Timothy Ogden and so much more. What a magical web he had woven into my life and how dull it would have been without him.

~

Monday came, and it was time for Dad's operation. Toddy rang to say he would be home later that day, and that things had gone well at The Pot of Gold, although something weird had happened and whatever I did I mustn't open any letters that arrived for me.

'But, Toddy! I can't promise that. I have to open my

business mail. How can I ignore them?' I asked, perplexed.

'Just open nothing!' he insisted. And hung up.

I had to go to the factory that day, despite my mind being occupied by Dad's operation. We had a delegation from America visiting, to see how we functioned and whether they would invest and copy our ideas for the good of the American people. The scientists had really come up with the goods and presented all the facts and figures in a most scientific way. Rory and Liam were top-notch and made me very proud. I smiled as I watched and remembered our trip to the land of the Grimms. They were truly dedicated to our cause.

The Americans were impressed and decided to take on our ideas and plans wholesale. They would also promote *The Plastic Dragon* and *The Last Oak Tree* stories. They could see a movie deal on the way, I told them any profit made from these must be channelled into the fight to save the planet and they agreed wholeheartedly.

It was a successful day all round, at work, that is.

When I checked my mail, there was the usual stack of invoices and promotion letters, and one postmarked from Ireland which looked curious. It had a stamp with the face of a leprechaun. I didn't know such a stamp existed, but thought it a quaint idea. I was about to open it, having completely forgotten Toddy's warning, when the phone rang. It was Mum to say the operation was over and it was now a waiting game to see how Dad responded. The next twenty-four hours were crucial and would I please come to the hospital? I thrust the leprechaun letter in my pocket and set off straight away. Mum was in the waiting room looking haggard and worried.

'I'm not sure what the doctors are trying to tell me, Donovan, but I get the sense that it's not good.'

'What do you mean?' I asked. I had been convinced that Conan would look after Dad, but now realised my fickleness. A higher power was involved in life and death issues. I'm sure Conan meant well, but perhaps he was trying to appease me.

I persuaded Mum to come to the hospital canteen and have a cup of tea. She looked dreadful and was silent. There was nothing much to say. We needed to channel our energy into positive thoughts for Dad.

Hospitals are such sanitary places, but I'm always

captivated by the nurses; they are special beings who put people at their ease in the most dire of situations. They know what to say and they are companions through suffering. The nurses looking after Dad were no exception. They tried to reassure us that Dad was not suffering and that if he held out the way he was things would be OK. There would be a slow path to recovery, but we must hope for the best.

We waited and waited. Lisa came for a while and brought a flask of tea and some sandwiches. It seemed dad was not out of the woods yet, and twice the docs thought we were losing him. I was dozing beside Dad's bed while he was attached to a lot of machinery. Mum was sleeping in a chair on the other side of the bed. I stirred for a moment and glanced up to see Conan. He looked solemn and watched my dad for a while, then looked at me and smiled and nodded reassuringly. Then he was gone.

A great sense of calm overcame me and I shifted in my chair and put my hands in my pocket where the letter lay. I pulled it out and once again mesmerised by the unusual stamp, began to open it, whereupon, Toddy rushed in.

'Stop! Don! Don't open it!' He grabbed me by the shoulders. 'Don, look at me! Look at me!' I looked at him in shock. Mum woke up, and we both thought Toddy was attacking me.

'Don I need you to answer this question with no thought or hesitation,' he said. 'Are you ready?'

I nodded.

'Right!' he said. 'Now look at your dad and answer this question.' I looked at Dad, laying there in such a bad way and the heart monitor faltered.

'Don, if you had one wish now what would it be?' Toddy asked. I looked at him incredulous that he could play such a game at this time. He tried the gentle approach; 'what would it be, Don? Look at your dad and tell me what you would wish for.'

I said, without further hesitation. 'I'd wish for my father to get better.' Toddy smiled. 'Then say it. Say the words!'

'I wish my father would get better.' Toddy hugged me so hard I felt my head would pop off my shoulders.

'Any chance of a cup of tea?' We froze, it was Dad, eyes open and alert.

He would pull through. The doctors came and were so amazed by his speedy recovery they allowed him to go home later that day. It was unbelievable! We were astonished but eternally grateful that Dad was back. We drove him and Mum home early evening and left them happily planning the stall for the next weekend. It really was remarkable.

When we returned to the cottage, Toddy was waiting for us at the gate. It was good to see Gretel again; our trusty companion along the fairy road, and I was eager to hear an explanation for Toddy's odd behaviour.

'Don, when I was at the Pot of Gold sorting out a few things, a little man appeared, not unlike Conan and Bronan.' I felt a story coming on, so settled down with a cool drink of orange juice, though nothing could have prepared me for what I was about to hear. He told me Conan had been in touch to say the bad ones were out to get you and me after our respective escapes from Ballymena. He said Conan gave you three wishes, and you'd already used two of them.'

WHAT?

I had no recollection of Conan giving me three wishes, or of making any wishes, come to think of it. Toddy continued; 'He said the bad one had sent you a letter and you must not open it under any circumstances. Conan could not interfere with your wishes, because he gave them to you, but it is OK to do it indirectly. That's when I rang you to tell you not to open a letter if one arrived, but there you were about to open it when I arrived in the nick of time! I suspected it was something to do with the wishes, and wanted to make sure you used your final wish on something that mattered to you, hence my behaviour, which I know was out of order under the circumstances, with your dad so sick, but I think it worked in a flash.'

I pondered this and nodded slowly. 'So what's in the envelope?' I mused, reaching for my jacket and pulling out the letter with the leprechaun stamp. Inside was a black page and written on it in large silver script were the words; I WISH I'D NEVER MET CONAN.

We were both stunned to silence as we contemplated the disastrous consequences, had I read the wish. We tracked everything that had happened before and after Toddy finding me at Glastonbury. It was obvious we had had a very narrow escape. I thanked Toddy for acting so swiftly and using his initiative.

'But Toddy for the life of me, I can't recall making two wishes.'

'I've been thinking about that. Remember when I told you how poor we were and would have to sell the house and live in Gretel?'

I nodded.

'You said; *"I wish you could find a pot of gold."* That was the week I inherited the Pot of Gold.' My jaw dropped. Then, I recalled my wish for more money to help the eco projects along, and the Americans came and the MP helped. How could I have missed Conan telling me I had three wishes? Must have been distracted. However, it all worked out for the best thanks to Toddy, Conan and Conan's Irish cousin.

Chapter 36

America Calls

After that, everything settled down to a normal routine, except not that normal. We three; you, your mum and I, bought a camper van and travelled to my future gigs together, and I always knew you saw the fairies, although I didn't want to mention it until you told me about them. I saw you playing with them in the garden one day when you were five years old. There were three fairies, and you were throwing autumn leaves around and having a lot of fun. It didn't surprise me since Conan and the Fairy Queen had touched your forehead that day as you slept in your crib.

The wood became your home, just as it had been for me and your grandma and great grandparents. Then we had to move away. It seemed the Universe had plans for us and America was calling.

My books were made into movies, the eco factory empire had expanded so much they needed me to put things in place over here and get the factory running the same efficient way as the England branch. We were very sad to leave our lives behind, but sometimes there seems no other way but to follow your instincts. We left the cottage in the wood and Ivanhoe, but always thought we would return. Toddy wrote a few times and said the woodland weekends had stopped happening because there was no organisation any more. That's the last I heard from him.

I carried on my storytelling gigs once I came here and Simon followed me. He's the Managing Director of the LA branch now.

As you know, your grandparents moved to America to

be close to us, and your Mum's folks moved to London.

So, my dear one, you asked me how I came to have a cottage in England and to tell you a bit about my life in Cotehill woods. I expect you thought I'd tell you it was dull as ditch water.

It was good to hear you went to visit the cottage and saw a fairy. I'd love to know more detail when you have the time to write. I know you're busy studying in London and now that I'm retired I have all the time in the world. I've enjoyed writing this down for you

Your Loving Dad.

Chapter 37

The E-mails

Dear Dad,

I've just finished reading about your life here in Cotehill wood. Yes, I'm still here, haven't left yet. I'm sorry I sent such a short note, but I was rushing to catch a train and then life got busy, as it usually does. When I reached Cotehill, it was exactly as you described it. The village hall. The Greyhound Inn and my grandparents' houses are all there. You wouldn't know twenty years had passed.

I found the woods from the map you gave me. They can't have changed much. They too are just as you described them. Lots of old trees and the little path I imagine you and Ivanhoe rode along. Dad, the most wonderful thing of all was seeing the cottage again. It is so overgrown and neglected, but the honeysuckle is still there, and I remembered you'd remarked on its lovely perfume. It hasn't changed. Thanks for sending the key. When I opened the door, you can imagine the cobwebs and dampness, but I almost cried when I saw the tiny furniture Seth made, and your big chair, and Mum's treadle sewing machine. It's all there, and I recalled things from my time here, although it wasn't long. I remembered the fairies in the garden and went outside to where we used to play. I remembered the story tent you talk about and the storyteller who made the stories so real and exciting. That must have been Toddy. Is he still here at Cotehill, I wonder? So, Dad I went to the supermarket and bought a stack of cleaning stuff, then set about making this place spick and span, the way it used to be.

Did you know you'd left Great, Great Granddad Seth's picture here? I guess because you thought you'd be back. It really feels like time stood still after you left. And guess what else I found beneath the overgrown brambles and covered with a tarpaulin? Ivanhoe! Yes! He's still here; been waiting all these years for you to come home. I've given him a polish and sent a pic. So now that I've told you about the cottage, I'll tell about the other stuff, Dad, as I mentioned, I cleaned the place up and bought some pretty bedding, so I could spend the night here. It worried me it might be creepy, but your account made me feel I knew everything I needed to know about the place and there's nothing bad to worry about. So I brought some books to study and my iPhone and a mini-speaker so I could listen to music. Electricity is lacking, but I found a few paraffin lamps while I was cleaning and got them going. Then I'm reading my book and listening to Coldplay when a little voice comes from behind me. I knew straight off it was Conan. 'Don boy's daughter!' he said. 'And looking every bit the beautiful angel you did when I saw you last.''And would you by any chance be Mr. Conan?' I asked. 'Conan, just call me Conan.' Can you believe it dad? I won't go into the full conversation, but he asked after you and told me what a brave lad you were back in the day, and how you'd saved the Cotehill Fairyland branch, just as you'd told me. I told him about your work in America to stem the tide of plastic waste worldwide and tour campaigns across the globe against the destruction of the rainforest and protecting wildlife. He said he's very proud of you, and hoped that one day you'd come back and live in Cotehill wood. Then, when evening fell, I could smell the night-scented stock and imagined you and mum at the table in the garden tucking into Grandma's quiche and then with Indigo, listening to the Bassenthwaite troupe.

I can't believe there's so much family history and magic in this wood, Dad. Then I remembered the fairy clean-up line and followed your directions. It wasn't long before I saw the glow and slowly crept towards it, but there was no need to creep because those fairies are so busy and still relentlessly clearing up, that they didn't seem to notice me. I watched them for ages, thinking about all the times you'd stood on exactly the same spot all those years ago, and how you wrote The Plastic Dragon because of them. You're amazing, Dad! I love you so much for that. After a while, I turned to go back to the cottage, but something made me wander deeper into the wood. I had my phone torch so could see just fine. I walked until... you know what I'm about to say. I walked until I saw a huge old oak tree and something told me it was the last oak tree. And so I walked beyond it, just as you did with Conan and Toddy, until everything changed and there was so much light, I didn't need the torch. I heard the singing, Dad, and then there was the fairyland tree, looking breathtakingly magical. On one of its branches sat a fairy wearing a bright red dress and smiling directly at me. 'Poppy?' I felt like crying, Dad, thinking about you here in this amazing, magical wood. 'Yes, it's me,' Poppy answered, 'I'm so happy you came back.' With that the place lit up so brightly my eyes were dazzled and the most fabulous fairy emerged from the tree. Long black hair and deep brown eyes, and wearing an aquamarine dress. I guessed she was the Fairy Queen. They danced and sang around me, and then she touched my forehead with her wand, the way she did when I was in the cradle, just as you told me. Eventually, they led me to the last oak tree, or as you said, it could be the first, depending how you look at it. They led me to the cottage, lighting the way and when I reached the gate, Poppy whispered in my ear. 'It's because you're Donovan's daughter. You are our Princess Fionuala.' That's exactly as it happened Dad, and thank goodness I know you'll believe me, because if I told anyone else they'd think I was going crazy.

I slept like a log and woke up to the sun peeping through my bedroom window. Tomorrow I have to go to London for the week, but hope to come back here for a while after that and write my thesis. I called in at the Carlisle Library, where mum worked, and they were very helpful in ordering the books I need. I'm going to send this email now, together with some pics I've taken of the cottage and the woods, oh and Ivanhoe. Give my love to Mum. Lots of love (Princess) Fionuala.

Dear Fionuala,

Your Mum and I wept when we read your email. It all sounds so familiar and we're thrilled you went to visit the cottage and made it spic and span. Poor Ivanhoe, I've had many dreams of him in his lonely and neglected state and the cottage. Your mention of the treadle and the honeysuckle evoked such sweet memories. Here, life continues in the same old, same old way. More high-rise apartment blocks and office blocks. More cars and fewer trees. I don't think anyone cares about the work we do, no matter how much we try, or how relentlessly we carry on there are so many people who prefer to ignore the warning signs. I'm getting tired now. Tired of the struggle, but then I hear about the Cotehill fairies and how they are still doing their thing after all this time, they haven't given up, so I guess I'll just carry on too. Your Mum is fine and Grandma and Granddad called round. They send their love. I mentioned you'd been to Cotehill, and they asked me to ask you to say hi to everyone. Can you believe that some people are denying climate change has anything to do with messing up the planet? And don't get me started on the Oceans, Fi. We need to start a campaign just for them. Take care in London. Your Loving Dad

Dear Dad,

I'm back at the cottage. London was fine, a huge contrast to the woods. I visited a few galleries and museums and got my thesis on track. I came back here yesterday. There's still no electricity but I'll see to that tomorrow, also I must sort out some wood for the stove. I guess I'll use your saw and axe. I called in at the Greyhound Inn and the landlady remembers you all. Said she was a kid when you and mum opened up the woods, and she would go along and listen to stories and read books about flowers and trees and woodland animals. She said it was so special, she's never forgotten those times. Sends her love to you and Grandma and Granddad. It was amazing to hear her story about your stories. Also the Blue Moon Club's still going. Believe it or not, there's a photo of you and Toddy together in your top hats playing the tin whistles. They have it in a frame on the wall behind the bar. I told them I'm your daughter, and we had a chat, The landlord's the same as when you were there, believe it or not...

The phone rings, interrupting her email:
 'Hello, Fi speaking.'
 'Hello Fionuala!'
 'Dad, hi I'm just about to send you an email...'
 'That's nice, but if you let us in I can read it now.'
 'I don't follow?'
 'The cottage door's just as I remember. If you open it you'll get a surprise.'
 'Mum! Dad! You're here!'

Prologue

Don and Lisa had returned to the cottage in the woods, after so long away. Fionuala cleared the cottage, which had been neglected, and buried in the brambles and soon it was cosy and inviting once again.

Donavan called on Toddy, who was ageing but still sprightly, and the two returned to the Blue Moon, where the landlord took a picture of them wearing the same hats and in the same pose as the one on the wall. He invited them back to tell their stories, and they happily accepted.

Lisa and Fionuala started the weekend wood gatherings again and baked the most wonderful cookies and muffins, which Lisa had learned to make in New York.

Simon followed them home after retiring from the LA Branch, and resumed his post as Gig Manager for Don and Toddy.

Grandma and Granddad returned to help with the woodland project.

Conan and Poppy often visited the cottage in the woods, and they all lived happily ever after.

THE END

Catherine of Liverpool
A Victorian Workhouse Tale
By Kathleen Boyle

ISBN: 978 1731136671

Into the City of Liverpool in 1876, torn by extremes of poverty and riches created by the Industrial Revolution and booming trade, Catherine Cattell was born. In 1888, she was admitted into the Liverpool Workhouse, together with her little brothers Billy and Alfie. Broken by the death of her mother, and the mysterious disappearance of her father John, Catherine begins a relentless battle to re-unite the shattered family. With the aid of faithful friends Bernadette and Colleen, and cousin Maude she finds the strength to survive the torturous workhouse regime, amidst rumours that her father has sailed to America on a ship called The Liverpool Lady. Beyond the workhouse the search for John continues, while Catherine works for Molly in her hat shop and Billy is lost at sea.

Printed in Great Britain
by Amazon